When I Was A Girl and Not Very Pretty

Hasna's Story

A Palestinian Saga

Book 1

Donn Hutchison

Text Copyright by Donn Hutchison c. 2015

Cover photograph by Anan Barghouti

ISBN: 978-0-9970990-1-0

First Edition

With love for Rana, Ramzi, and Kahlid always, and in loving memory of my Palestinian mother-in-law, Ellen Audi Mansur, who was born during the last decade of the Ottoman rule, who was a teacher, wife and mother during the British Mandate, and was a *gifted storyteller.*

Contents

Chapter 1

In her seventeen years of marriage, Im Issa had *'swallowed a fly'* seventeen times; that's what the old women in the village called *conception*. Out of those seventeen *'swallowings'*, there had been sixteen bloody nights where she *'sat on a stone'* in a circle of bloody dirt; two strong neighbor women pressing against her back, a third raising her arms above her head, the midwife kneeling at her feet with rags in her hands to catch the infant before its head hit the stone.

The baby's head never hit the stone, but ten of those infants had died within their first year anyway. It was the *will of Allah,* so the neighbor women said, though secretly they whispered to each other: *I wonder what Im Issa did to be so cursed?*

Salma had been married off at fourteen. Her husband, Abdallah, was thirty-four when they married and from a neighboring village. It was somewhat uncommon for a girl to be married to a man from a different *clan,* almost unheard of to be married to a man from a different *village.*

It had happened in a strange way – *but so it was written* – her mother had said. Abdallah was a master builder and had been brought to supervise the building of the *mukhtar's* house. Salma, along with many girls from the village, had been drafted into carrying water to the builders who made the mortar. Abdallah, who had been recently widowed, had seen her. He had asked the *mukhtar* about her and had persuaded the village leader to introduce him to the girl's father.

Salma was one of many daughters. A man was *blessed* if he had sons, not *so-blessed* if he had a houseful of daughters. A man's house was made strong with sons – his *line* was secure; a girl remained in her father's house only until she married, and then she became the *property* of her husband and built up *his house.*

Salma's father looked at the man who had come to ask for his daughter. He was rich by village standards; a widower with grown children. He had readily agreed to the bride price that Salma's father had asked, and had promised generous gifts to him and his brothers. The fact that he was twenty years older than Salma was of no consequence.

Even after seventeen years of marriage, her wedding was a blur. Oh, there were some things that she remembered: *being swathed in veils, carrying a sword in front of her face to ward off the evil spirit, trying to keep astride the camel that carried her from her village to that of her husband.* She remembered her mother-in-law, she guessed it must have been her mother-in-law, placing a piece of dough in her hands and telling her to press it above the lintel. She *did* remember her husband slapping her hand three times in the symbol of *obedience.*

There was one thing she wished she could forget – *the deflowering.* Her husband had *bribed* her with coins. When he felt he had given her a sufficient number, he had forced himself upon her. She remembered *too well* crying and wanting to scream as he lifted her skirt, covered her mouth with his hand, and *thrust* into her. He had claimed his right several more times that night.

When he had rolled off her the last time and finally slept, she had inched her battered body to the side of the pallet and wept. She had not thought it would be like this.

In the morning she had presented her spotted chemise to her mother-in-law – *proof* that she had been a virgin – *proof* that she had been *deflowered.* Her mother-in-law had handed her a pitcher and told here where the village well was. She had said: *"Inshallah, you have 'swallowed a fly' and will provide my son with a boy!"* Abdallah had gone off to the coffeehouse to swagger and boast that he had successfully *deflowered* the bride.

Salma had been pregnant every year for seventeen years. She had borne sixteen children and was pregnant with the seventeenth! Her three oldest had been boys, *illhumdillah- Praise God,* Issa, Khalil, and Awad. Last year, Issa who was 16 and Khalil who was 15 had been conscripted into the Turkish Army. The news had been brought by a neighbor boy who had been drafted with them and discharged when he lost his right arm; Issa and Khalil had died in a place called *Shana Kala* in Turkey. They had one remaining son, Awad, and two girls: Helweh and Henneh – *three out of sixteen!*

At thirty-one, she was heavy with child again; life had been hard when she was a girl, but then everyone's life had been hard; but life as a married woman had made her bitter! She was always referred to as *'the outsider'* even though she had lived with her husband's family in his village for seventeen years, and her own village was only ten miles away; her mother-in-law was a harsh, complaining, critical woman – *nothing* Salma did was ever right; her husband was a difficult, domineering, *demanding* man who *blamed her* for the deaths of their infants. She had once told him that the midwife had *suggested* that she *rest* between pregnancies, that having babies only ten months apart was perhaps partially to blame for them not surviving. He had slapped her and accused her of *questioning what had been written.* Salma felt *cursed* by God. Oh, she mouthed the right words: *illhumdillah- praise God, zay ma Allah Bid-do- it is as God wills, Nush'kerallah- our thanks to God* – but she and God were no longer on speaking terms.

Salma went into labor with her seventeenth child early in the morning. The pains had been severe from the beginning. Abdallah had gone off to the coffeehouse when her labor had begun, only telling her, *Inshallah, you give me a son.* Her sister-in-law had gone to call the midwife – the same old woman, well-past menopause who had delivered her sixteen previous babies; she also brought back with her two neighbor women to assist in the delivery.

They had carried into the dark room, where she and Abdallah slept with their three children, a flat stone for her to sit on, a basket of dirt to spread on the floor around the stone to catch the blood, a bundle of rags, a bottle of olive oil, and an earthenware bowl of salt.

Her labor seemed to go on and on and on. Her body was worn out from the continual pregnancies; her heart was broken over the death of her two sons. She knew better than to *scream* or *moan.* She had screamed with the first child – seventeen years ago, and had been *scolded* by the women who had attended her. Her mother-in-law had held her hand over her mouth when she screamed; "*You mustn't disturb my son and shame him and us by your screaming,*" she had rasped. The midwife cautioned that her screaming would *harm the baby.* Her mother-in-law had told her that *good women had a short labor and an easy delivery; mean women suffered.* Salma thought that she must have been very mean, but she couldn't figure out what she had done. She had not screamed or moaned. She had bitten her lips until they bled. She suffered. She was not yet fifteen years old.

Salma *endured* as she had *endured* for seventeen years. After eight hours of hard labor, the midwife could finally see the head. The neighbor women braced their strong backs against Salma's back. Salma raised herself from the stone on which she sat on trembling legs. Her sister-in-law, Miriam, raised Salma's arms above her head, and the midwife told her to give one powerful push. She did. The midwife *caught* the baby before the baby's head could hit the stone. She grabbed the baby by its feet and slapped it soundly. She laid the bloody infant on Salma's chest; the umbilical cord was still attached.

Salma looked at the robust infant – probably the biggest of all the babies she had borne. The midwife looked away and said, "Im Issa, it's a girl."

"Abu Issa will not be pleased. He had wanted a boy. I have failed him yet again." She looked down at this her seventeenth child. "Not only is it a girl, but she has *red* hair," she sighed. "He will not be pleased."

The midwife cut the cord and tied off the stump. She handed the infant to Miriam to clean. The blood was wiped from the infant with a rag. Miriam massaged olive oil into the sturdy limbs; over the back and buttocks, over the head and face. She then worked salt into the oil to make the infant hardy. The baby was then swaddled in rags; her arms were pressed close to her torso; her legs were straightened; around the rags a strip of cloth was wound and tied. All that was left exposed was her face and her head with its fuzzy red hair. Miriam placed the baby on a straw tray.

Salma's body did not want to expel the afterbirth. The midwife tied a string about the stump of cord still attached to the afterbirth; she then tied the string around Salma's big toe. She put a handful of pepper under Salma's nose and said, "Sneeze and stretch out your foot!"

Salma did; she pulled the afterbirth out. The midwife caught it in a rag and put it in a basket. Miriam swept up the bloody dirt and put it on top of the rag containing the afterbirth. It was taken outside and buried. The neighbor women carried the stone out of the house.

The midwife went to the coffeehouse to tell Abdallah that he had a daughter. She stood away from the seated men and called. "Abu Issa, *Blessed is the bride.*"

He hollered back, "I do not pay for the birth of a girl." He went on playing backgammon with his friend.

Salma lay in a stupor. She was exhausted. She was disappointed – *if she had only had a son, Abdallah would have been pleased. He would not be pleased with a girl – a girl with red hair.* The only thing that gave her a bit of comfort was that for *forty days* she would be unclean. For forty days she would sleep alone; custom was strict about a man not approaching his wife during this period of time.

Automatically, she put the infant to her breast and guided a nipple into its mouth. She had to admit that the little one seemed to be smart, in that as soon as the nipple touched her lips she latched on and started to suck. Salma ran a rough, work worn palm over the fuzzy red hair. "How unfortunate that you are a girl; how unfortunate that you have red hair; you will have to be strong, if you are to survive," she whispered.

Salma's sister-in-law, Miriam, came into the room. "What are you going to call the girl?" she asked.

"I've named her *Hasna.*"

Chapter 2

Hasna was tenacious of life. She would lie on the straw tray, imprisoned in her cocoon of rags and solemnly observe the world through startling blue eyes – *evil* eyes some peasants thought. The only times she was picked up were when Salma nursed her or changed the soiled rags. She didn't cry, as cries were ignored. She couldn't kick her feet or move her hands as they were bound tightly to her body. All she could move was her head with its crown of red fuzz.

For the first forty days, Hasna had slept with her mother. Whenever she was hungry, her mother was right there and would ease a nipple into the searching mouth. She only needed to whimper, and immediately a nipple was between her lips. *You mustn't cry, Hasna, and awaken your father; you mustn't cry; hush, hush,* her mother had whispered.

Abdallah kept track of the forty days. It was one of the things he disliked about the arrival of a new baby -this forced period of abstinence; he sometimes dreamt of taking a second wife. He *knew* to the day when Salma could return to his pallet. He would surreptitiously watch her nurse the new baby; her breasts were full; the nipples prominent; he felt a stirring beneath his worn *umbaz.*

"Tonight you return to my pallet, Im Issa," he said leering at her. "Let the baby sleep beside Helweh and Henneh."

Salma nodded her head and said nothing. It would begin again.

That night he was upon her as soon as she slid beneath the comforter. He never said anything. He pushed up her skirt and brutally entered her; he would fondle her full breasts; his moustache and beard left brush burns on her flesh as he *nursed*. When this had first happened, seventeen years ago, he had whispered to her: *a woman's milk is good for a man – it makes him virile.* She had no way of knowing if this was normal or not *–did all husbands do this?* Talk about what happened between a woman and a man was taboo. She endured his lips sucking on her breast. Her hands lay at her sides; the fingers drawn into fists. He moved and sucked and moaned in pleasure. She hated him.

Once, years ago when one of her infants had died and her breasts were full with milk, a neighbor woman had expired in childbirth. Her infant son had survived, but needed a wet nurse. The husband had broached the subject with *Abdallah*. He had asked *Abdallah* if he would allow Im Issa, since their baby had died, to be a wet nurse for his baby as its mother had died. Abdallah refused. Salma had ventured to tell him that since her breasts were full and painful, she would be willing to nurse the orphan infant. She would never forget what he said. *The milk in your breasts is not yours. It is mine to do with as I please.* During the day, when Abdallah was out of the house, she bound her breasts tightly with cloth bindings so the milk would dry up. She removed them before nightfall when he would be once again upon her.

Salma had grudgingly learned from her mother-in-law how to make the *khabiyeh* – the storage bins constructed of mud and straw that separated the one-room living quarters from the narrow storage area. The *khabiyeh* were tall separate units open from the top. There was a small hole at the bottom to let the grain out. A rag was wedged in the hole to keep it closed. The unit was used to store the year's supply of: wheat, lentils, barley, dried figs, and raisins. Once they were constructed and allowed to dry in the sun, men carried them into a house and placed them on the *mastabeh*— the upper level where the family lived. The units were then whitewashed and often had designs painted on them. Salma had an artist's hand, and the primitive designs she painted on the *khabiyeh* were much sought after. Abdallah would *allow* her to occasionally decorate the *khabiyeh*; he always expected a coin in payment. She was allowed to do nothing without his permission.

There was only *one* thing in the house that belonged to her. It was the *sanduq al urus* – the wooden bridal chest she had brought with her from her father's home. It had a key and was kept locked. Even Abdallah had *no right to open it.* Her bridal chest was empty, except for the embroidered dress she had worn for her wedding. Nevertheless, she kept it *locked.* It was as though the *emptiness* within was *hers* and not Abdallah's.

The lower level of the house, the *qa'albayt*, was where the goats and sheep were penned at night. The few chickens they had hid their eggs in the straw, and it was the job of ten-year old Helweh and nine-year old Henneh to search each morning for eggs. The plow, when not in use, was housed there as were primitive rakes and spades.

The low wooden door of the house opened to the *qa'albayt*; to the left were stone steps that lead to the upper level where the family slept. There was only one, tall, barred window between the two levels; it let the only light into the house which didn't come in through the open door. Most of the work was done outside in the courtyard. To be inside the house was to move in shadows. *It is much like my life,* Salma thought, if she ever really thought about it. *This was the lot of women to move in the shadows, to be vessels of a man's lust, to tend to his needs, to give him sons, to never complain, and hopefully to die and one day finally rest.*

As she went down the stone stairs one morning a black snake slithered across the bottom step and disappeared into the straw. She hollered at Helweh and Henneh, "Come and search for the eggs now. That old, black snake will be finding them before you do and sucking them dry."

"What about Hasna?" Helweh called. "What shall we do with her?"

"Bring her down in her wooden box and set her in the shade next to the *zir* (the water jug)."

So Hasna was carried down in her box and put under the shade of the gnarled fig tree where she could stare at the sun filtering through the leaves. She couldn't move her hands to try and catch the snatches of sun; she couldn't kick from joy at being out in the fresh air; she could only lie on her back and ponder the world of the fig tree through her thoughtful, *foreign-colored* eyes.

Salma was strict with her two daughters. Helweh and Henneh *never* could recall that their mother had ever smiled. She was always sharp and critical of them, just as their grandmother had been. She was constantly ordering and scolding: *That's not the way to gather eggs; why did you take so long in fetching the water; go and collect brush for the fire; bring the mattresses down to air; go and collect wild greens; see to the stew in the kiddreh; don't speak unless you are spoken to.*

It wasn't that Salma disliked her girls; she didn't. She supposed, at some level, she loved them. As an *outsider,* she felt she had to be even stricter with her daughters. They *must* be taught to be: *industrious, obedient, and pleasant; to be modest, to have good characters, to not bring dishonor to their father, and to eventually be good wives, mothers, and daughters-in-laws.* She truly believed that a daughter must never be *pampered;* a *pampered* daughter disgraces a family; a *pampered* son, however, makes a man rich!

Awad, at fourteen, was pampered and spoiled. Oh, he did take the sheep and goats to the fields and went with his father to learn how to be a master builder, but at home he sat with the men; his sisters waited on him hand-and-foot; he ordered them about as though he were a *prince* and they were his personal servants. At an early age, he learned that they were *inferior,* and daily thanked God that he had been born a boy.

Once he had broken an earthenware bowl. His mother, seeing the broken bowl, *slapped* his sister, Helweh, who was standing beside him. Helweh didn't protest; he didn't confess. That was just the way it was. He was a boy and could *do no wrong;* Helweh was *only* a girl.

Where Helweh and Henneh were faded prints of the dark beauty that was once their mother's, Hasna was an unbecoming throwback to some Scottish Crusader. Even as a toddler, she stood out with her bright red hair and deep blue eyes. Heads would turn when she was carried on her mother's shoulder; heads would turn when her sisters held her hands and she took tentative steps across the cobblestones; heads would turn and unspoken questions were thought: *From where had this aberrant child come?*

When Hasna started to talk well, she tended to say whatever came to her mind. Once she was sitting on the stone steps leading to the *mastabeh,* watching the sheep and goats file into the *qa'albayt;* her sister Henneh was counting them as they leaped over the stone threshold, a newborn lamb had put trembling, spindly legs onto the threshold, but couldn't push itself over. It was black; all the rest of the sheep and lambs were wooly white. The older ewes would push the lamb aside with their heads and jump over the threshold.

"Why are the mothers doing that?" Hasna asked.

"They don't want to accept the lamb because she is different." Henneh answered.

The black wooly lamb stood on its wobbly legs and bleated mournfully. One of the ewes kept turning her head and looking in the direction of the bleating lamb. Henneh reached down and picked the lamb up and took it to the ewe. She set it down. At first the ewe would butt it with her head and turn around. Henneh moved the lamb beneath the ewe so it could suck. The ewe would move away. Henneh persisted and finally, reluctantly, the ewe stood still long enough for the lamb to begin to nurse.

"She'll allow her to nurse now." Henneh said.

"But she doesn't really want her, does she?" Hasna asked.

"No, but she's its mother; as long as she doesn't have to look at it, she can *pretend* that it is white."

"Like *Im'me* (my mother) has to *pretend* when she looks at me," Hasna sighed.

The rule of survival in a small village was to *blend in,* to be *exactly* like everyone else. It is hard to *blend in* when one has *red hair and blue eyes.* Hasna was dressed exactly like the other children in drab, worn, threadbare garments. Her feet were bare, calloused on the bottom and dirty, just like the other children's. Her hair was braided and tied with a bit of string, just like that of other girls her age. She *sounded* like the other children, but unfortunately, she *didn't* look like the other children.

The rare occasions when the girls her age would be playing, she was always excluded. She stood on the sidelines and watched, *hoping* they would include her. Sometimes she would force her way into a game, and would be pushed out. *We don't want you, Hasna. You stand over there and watch, or better still go home.*

"I don't want to play with you, anyway!" she would shout, lying to herself and to them.

Hasna compensated by being very good at whatever she set her hand to. She was clever and only had to be told once how to do something. She was a hard worker and could *see* what needed to be done *before* she was told. She became quite skilled at embroidery. *She would be a perfect daughter,* Salma thought, *if she didn't have blue eyes, red hair, and freckles.*

Chapter 3

By the time Hasna was six, her sisters, Helweh and Henneh, were both married. The work that they had done now became *her* work to do. It seemed she was in constant motion from morning until she went to bed at dusk. She drove the animals out of the *qa'albayt* in the morning; she gathered the eggs finding them before the black snake could sink his fangs into the shells and suck them dry. She once asked her mother *why the black snake was not caught and killed. Her mother had told her the snake was good for catching mice and couldn't help having a fondness for chicken eggs.*

She carried the pallets, almost as big as she was, outside and wrestled them to the top of a stone wall so they could be saturated with sun. She squatted before an enamel basin and washed dishes, setting them in the sun to dry. She sat opposite her mother when wheat was ground on the stone mill; their worn, patched skirts pushed up to their knees; their bare feet almost touching as they turned the wooden handle that moved the top stone against the bottom, pulverizing the grains of wheat that had been funneled into the small hole in the top. Her mother gave her small pieces of dough to work as Hasna learned to make bread. She learned to carry heavy bundles on her head: tins of water from the well, bundles of brush so large that when she carried them back to the village it looked as though the bundle had legs.

Her mother insisted that she constantly tie a large kerchief about her head so that as much of her red hair as possible was covered. Unfortunately, she couldn't cover the color of her eyes, or the freckles that had started to splotch her skin.

Hasna took care of her two little brothers, often going about her work with a small child on her hip; she was only six! She dressed in drab, patched rags like her mother. She wore a once-white head shawl, like her mother's, when she went outside the courtyard. It was long enough to hide her red braids. She kept her eyes downcast so people wouldn't readily see that her eyes were blue.

Salma would look at her daughter and sigh. *She is such a hard worker, but she is not pretty. Perhaps some old man will take her for a second wife. In the dark, he won't see her red hair, blue eyes and freckles.* Every time she looked at Hasna, she had another reason to be *upset with God.*

Hasna's two little brothers, Saif and Ali, adored her. As busy as she was, she seemed to always have time to play with them, to carry them about. They would see her pass and lift up their arms to be carried, even though they were both big enough to walk.

Salma would scold her. *Put that little one down! You have work to do! They are big enough to play on their own!* The two little boys trailed after Hasna wherever she went. She went to gather brush, and they were there holding onto her raggedy skirt. They would sit on a stone step and watch her drive the sheep and goats out of the lower level of the house. Sometimes they would get down and pretend to shoo the lambs out too. When the family gathered around the large straw tray to eat, there would be Saif and Ali sitting on either side of Hasna. She would hand chunks of bread she'd dipped in the stew to them. At night, it was Hasna who would put them to bed on a pallet next to hers. They weren't old enough to realize that *she was different*.

Her sister-in-law was.

Awad, at twenty, had married a girl of sixteen. Miryam was plump and comely. She had thick raven braids that hung to her knees. She outlined her black eyes with *kohl*. Her dusky skin was without blemish. She had small, even white teeth. On a nail, next to her bridal chest, she had hung a mirror. Miryam would often gaze at herself, twist a stray hair into place; moisten her lips. Awad was infatuated. He conveniently overlooked the fact that Miryam was lazy.

Oh, she wasn't lazy if Salma was looking, then she would *appear* to be industriously at work. When Salma *wasn't* looking she would take her time in doing whatever she was doing. *Hasna, come and help me with this. Hasna, go and fetch that. Hasna, where are you?*

If Hasna didn't move fast enough, or if Hasna didn't do her bidding, Miryam would complain to Awad. *I worked hard all day and your sister didn't help me at all. I would call her, and ask her oh, so sweetly, to do something for me, and she wouldn't listen.* Awad would scold Hasna or even box her ears.

When this happened, Miryam would look slyly at Hasna and pound her right hand into her left palm – gesturing *I showed you!* Awad didn't see, but Hasna did.

When Miryam and Hasna were alone, Miryam was horrible. *You really are quite ugly, you know?* Miryam would say. *You will never get married. What man is going to want a wife with red hair, horrible splotches on her face, and 'evil' blue eyes? You will be a servant in your father or brother's house until you die.*

Hasna never said anything. After all, she was only six and afraid of Miryam. Hasna never talked to anyone, except perhaps to Saif and Ali. She *never* complained to her mother. Salma didn't really see Hasna as a *child*. She saw her as a worker, a servant, someone who did what she was told.

In all six years of her life, she could not recall even *once* her father directly talking to her. She could *never* recall him ever calling her by name. He always referred to her as *the binit* – the girl. *Perhaps he doesn't know my name,* she thought. He didn't refer to her as *my* daughter, or *our* daughter; it was always just *the girl.*

As Hasna got older she took over more and more of the work. Once Miryam had had her first child, she became impossible. Miryam felt that motherhood, especially being the mother of a *son,* made her somewhat *removed* from doing ordinary chores. Salma would not have allowed her to get away with this attitude, if it hadn't been for Awad.

Awad is not his father's son, Salma thought. Where she had always been under Abdallah's thumb, the thumb pressing on Awad *was Miryam's.* Miryam was all sweetness in front of Salma and Abdallah. She would even joke with Abdallah and *tease him.* Abdallah was flattered and taken in by Miryam's coquettishness. He would sigh to himself and think: *Why couldn't I have had a wife like Miryam? She is a wife fit for the prophet himself.*

He would glance over at Salma; she had borne nineteen children; she was still slender, but her breasts sagged; her hair was threaded with gray; she never joked, or teased, or even *smiled!* He thought of the old proverb about the man who had two wives: *Sleeping by the old one is to me like an oven filled with dung! Sleeping by the new one is to me like the eve of God's feast.* Since the end of the war, the ousting of the Ottomans and the advent of the British, there was not much money to be had. He couldn't *afford* a second wife – at least not at the moment – but when he *could* he wanted a young wife, a girl of fifteen or sixteen – a girl like Miryam to warm his bed, a new *field in which to push his plow.* He smiled to himself as he felt the familiar stirring between his legs.

Awad would allow no criticism of Miryam. Abdallah would allow no criticism of Miryam. If there was *anyone* to be criticized, *it was twelve-year old Hasna!*

"Hasna, my son needs his wrappings changed. Come and do it!" Miryam commanded.

"Do it yourself." Hasna answered.

"*What did you say?*" Miryam screamed. "You come here, *right now,* and change this baby's wrappings, or I will tell Awad and *Ammie* Abdallah!"

"Tell them," Hasna smiled, her blue eyes looking directly into Miryam's dark eyes. "Tell them, and I will curse you. Your hair will fall out, your teeth will rot; you'll get spots on your face like mine!"

Miryam stammered, "What? You can't curse me!"

"Can't I? You are always saying '*Hasna, you are ugly. Hasna, you have evil eyes.*' Perhaps I *can* curse you. How will you know?" Hasna smiled knowingly. She knew Miryam was gullible. "Tell them, and see what happens."

Miryam *did* start to tell Awad at dinner. "I asked Hasna today to change the baby's wrappings and..."

Hasna looked directly at her and smiled as she rubbed a finger slowly at the side of her blue eye.

"And?" Awad asked.

"And she refused!" Miryam said with more bravado than she felt.

Abdallah, who was within arm's reach of Hasna, cuffed her along the side of the head. "You do what your sister-in-law says!"

Saif and Ali, who were sitting on either side of Hasna, moved as though they would protest what had happened but Hasna grabbed both of their arms and shook her head. Salma, for perhaps the first time in her married life, felt the twitch of a smile at the corners of her mouth as she looked at Hasna.

That evening, as Miryam was running a comb through her unbraided hair, she gasped to see the teeth of the comb full of strands of black hair. She turned to where Hasna lay on her pallet. Hasna was sitting up in bed, looking directly at her and smiling. She was rubbing a finger at the corner of her eye. Hasna raised her left palm and held it out; she slowly pounded her right fist into the open palm; *I'll show you,* the gesture said.

Chapter 4

The harvesting of barley and wheat took place in the spring and involved the entire family. The men and boys cut the grain with short-handled scythes; the women and children gathered the stalks of cut barley or wheat into bundles which were carried to the threshing floor.

Hasna worked tirelessly; bending and combing the cut stalks with her hands; twisting a bent stalk around a bundle then leaving it for Saif and Ali to pick up and carry to the side of the field. Her back was sore; sweat poured into her eyes and dripped off her face; her fingers were calloused and cracked. She worked uncomplainingly, humming to herself a song without words.

She made a game for Saif and Ali out of picking up the tied bundles and carrying them to the side of the field.

"How many have you carried *Saif habeebee* (my love)? How many have you carried, *habeebee*, Ali? I have a surprise for the one who has carried the most!" she said smiling at her two little brothers.

The boys couldn't read or write, but they *could* count. They had counted the sheep and goats with Hasna when she let them out in the morning and brought them back into the *qa'albayt* in the evening. They had counted the number of buckets of water it took to fill the earthenware jug that Hasna carried on her head from the well. They had counted the number of eggs in Hasna's basket when she outwitted the black snake and gathered the eggs before it got a chance to suck them dry. Some evenings they sat with Hasna on the domed roof of their house and tried to count the stars. Her arm would be around each of them; they would lean against her; their dark eyes reflecting starlight as they turned their faces to the heavens.

The only real affection they had was from Hasna. If they stumbled and fell, it was Hasna who kissed the hurt and brushed the dirt from their knees. If they had bad dreams at night, it was Hasna who rubbed their backs and held them in her lap and whispered soothing words into their ears as she kissed their curls. Whenever they looked at Hasna, she *smiled* at them. Their mother *never* smiled; their father *rarely* smiled; Awad and his wife *ignored* them. It *was* only Hasna who showed them love and called them *habeebee*.

Miryam complained as she gathered the stalks and made a bundle. She would rest a hand on her back and sigh – especially if Awad was near enough to *hear* her sigh and *see* her hand against her aching back. Gathering the cut stalks blistered her fingers and jabbed her toes. She moved slowly, *reluctantly,* through the field of cut wheat. She hated harvesting the grain.

Once all the stalks had been gathered into bundles, the bundles were carried to the threshing floor. The threshing floor was a large, relatively flat surface of natural stone. The bundles of wheat were placed on the floor and a team of mules was driven around, and around, and across the bundles to loosen the grain from the stalks.

The straw stalks were raked up and piled on the backs of donkeys and mules to be taken to the village and used by the women and girls in the weaving of baskets, as animal feed, as fuel for the oven and in the making of clay braziers, pots, vessels for water, and the *khabiyeh*. Nothing was wasted.

After the mules had loosened the grains from the stalks, women beat the grain with heavy wooden clubs to thresh the grain more finely. Then the men winnowed the threshed grain by throwing the wheat into the air using wooden pitchforks. There was almost a rhythm to their dance. They bent and picked up a forkful of grain; they tossed the grain into the air and the wind separated the grain from the chaff. They bent again and picked up a forkful of wheat, moving slightly to the right. Again, the wind separated the grain from the chaff.

When all the wheat had been winnowed, the women and girls *sifted* the grain to remove any small pebbles and bits of straw using large wooden sieves. The sifted grain was then scooped into cloth sacks which were roughly sewn shut with twine. The sacks were carried back to the village on the heads of the women and girls, who would then scoop the sifted wheat from the sacks into the *khabiyeh*.

It was backbreaking, exhausting work. The sack that Hasna carried on her head was so large that the end of it kept bumping her waist. She held on tightly to the ends of the sack to keep it balanced on her head. She was so soaked with sweat that the ends of her braids dripped water. She kept blinking the sweat out of her eyes. Her red eye lashes were heavy with chaff.

She saw her married sisters, Helweh and Henneh, in the distance. They too, with necks straining, were balancing heavy sacks of grain on their heads. Salma was walking ahead of her, back erect, two hands securing the heavy sack to her head. It was only Miryam who walked unburdened back toward the village. Hasna wondered what Miryam had said to Awad, or to her father, to get out of not carrying a heavy sack of grain on her head.

A slow donkey walked in front of her. It was so loaded with straw that all that could be seen were the donkey's four spindly legs. On top of the stack rode Saif and Ali. Hasna had to grin at the picture of her two little brothers perched on top of the mountain of straw. She could hear their laughter and imagine their smiles.

It was Hasna who perched on the top of the rickety ladder and poured the bowls of wheat, her mother and brothers handed her, into the top of the *khabiyeh*. The wheat crop had been good this year. After the *khabiyeh* was filled, there was still wheat left over to store in clay vessels in the *qa'albayt*.

"You worked hard today, *binti*," Abdallah said addressing Miryam.

Miryam smiled coyly at her father-in-law behind heavily-sooted lashes. "I only did what a good daughter-in-law would do, *Ammie*."

Abdallah smiled at her and felt a stirring in his worn *umbaz*.

Salma looked at Hasna; Hasna looked at her mother. Abdallah had *praised* Miryam; Abdallah had called Miryam *binti -'my daughter';* Abdallah had completely ignored Salma and Hasna who – of the three women – had done all the work.

Spring slid into summer – the time for harvesting the fruit. The fig tree in the courtyard was heavy with plump green figs. Saif and Ali were agile enough to climb high into the branches and pick the luscious fruit. They would fill their baskets and then, like monkeys, move from branch to branch until they could get low enough to swing their filled baskets to Hasna, who took them and handed up empty ones.

Salma stood on the ground and with a long pole pulled the branches down so Hasna could carefully pick the fruit and place it in her basket. Awad, at the other side of the tree, had placed a ladder against the branches and was filling a basket held up to him by Miryam. It didn't take long for the six of them to strip the tree of ripe fruit.

The figs were spread out in raked soil to dry. They were carefully arranged so that they did not touch one another. It took about five days for them to become fairly dry. They would then be packed tightly in tall wooden boxes and stored behind the *khabiyeh* for winter.

During the grape season in late summer, some members of the family moved to stone watchtowers (qasr) in the vineyards outside the village to guard against thieves and wild animals. The white grapes were especially good for the making of raisins. Hasna, Saif and Ali carefully stripped the individual grapes from the cluster, leaving a tiny stem on each grape. Salma coated each grape with a little olive oil and the grapes were left to dry in the sun. When the grapes were brown and wrinkled, Saif and Ali removed the tiny stem from each grape and the raisins were stored in wooden boxes for winter.

The ripe blue grapes were used in the making of *dibs* – molasses. Men from the village made the *dibs* using an abandoned wine-press. The grapes were placed on the floor of the wine press and large stone slabs were placed over them. Young men would stamp on the stone slabs with their bare feet, crushing the grapes. The juice would flow into sloping, rock-carved basins which emptied into a stone receptacle. The men would ladle the juice into metal containers that were placed over an open fire to boil. The juice was left to boil until it was the consistency of syrup. The impurities were skimmed off the top and discarded. After the juice had cooled, it was poured into brown-tinted bottles, corked and stored in the space behind the *khabiyeh.*

Some of the ripe grapes were put into bottles and allowed to ferment into vinegar.

It was when the majority of the family was in the vineyard that it happened. Miryam had not been feeling well, or so she had said, and had told Awad that she was going back to the house to rest.

"I won't be long. Little Abdallah is sleeping in the shade of the brush canopy of the *qasr;* I'll be back before he awakens," Miryam said.

Awad nodded abstractly at her and returned to picking the grapes. Salma watched her go and wondered *how* she always managed to get out of work.

Once Miryam was out of sight of the pickers, she was *miraculously* better. Her gait quickened as she approached the house. *It will be wonderful to have an hour all to myself,* she thought. She climbed the stone stairs to the *mastabeh,* removed her head shawl and knelt on her pallet in front of the mirror which dangled on its nail above her bridal chest.

She had unbraided her hair and was running her long, tapered fingers through the raven tresses. She looked into the mirror to admire her reflection when she saw him!

Her heart leaped into her throat, *"Ammie!"* she cried, fumbling to braid her hair. "I didn't know anyone was here."

He only smiled as he unwound the cloth girdle around his waist. Miryam picked up her head shawl and hastily covered her head. Her knees were trembling; her hands were shaking; she made for the stone steps but Abdallah blocked her way. He was still smiling as he moved closer and closer with outstretched arms.

"I have seen the way you look at me;" he softly sad, "the way you *tease* me."

"*Ammie,* I don't know what you mean! I am *your son's wife!*" she cried in desperation.

He had just placed his calloused hands on her arms and was forcing her down onto the pallet when a voice behind them said, "Miryam, *Im'me* sent me to fetch you. Little Abdallah is awake and wants to be nursed."

Abdallah and Miryam, both startled, turned to see twelve-year old Hasna standing at the top of the stone stairs.

"Miryam will be there in awhile," Abdallah rasped. "Go on! Go!"

Hasna just stood there.

"I *told you to go!*" her father shouted.

Hasna remained as though she had been carved from stone. Miryam hastily ran down the stairs and out the door.

Hasna couldn't move. *She wanted to move; she wanted to run; her legs were dead.*

Abdallah straightened his *umbaz* and slowly retied the cloth girdle around his waist. As he passed her, he stopped. He looked into her cold blue eyes, at her freckled face and red hair.

"*One word* and I will *kill you,*" he said. "Do you understand?"

Hasna only nodded. She understood *perfectly*. What she *would do* with that understanding was another matter.

Chapter 5

Late summer slipped into fall. Ever since the incident between Abdallah and his daughter-in-law, there was an inexplicable tension in the house – *inexplicable* to Salma and Awad that is; clear as spring water to Miryam, Abdallah, and Hasna.

For once in her married life, Miryam was *thankful* that she had no privacy. She no longer *innocently* flirted with her father-in-law. When she spoke to him, she lowered her eyes and mumbled her response. She realized that her flirtatiousness and coquettishness had lit a dangerous flame in her father-in-law.

Abdallah was *obsessed.* Miryam and Awad had been married six years and there was only *one* child. *Awad must be shooting water in which no fish swim,* he thought. Miryam *needed* a man *like Abdallah – a real man.* If anyone was to blame for his attraction to Miryam, *it was Miryam!* She had bewitched him. She really was *bitjenin* –her beauty could drive a person insane. Her beauty and accessibility *had* driven *him crazy.*

The fact that the Quran strictly forbade any kind of sexual relationship between a man and his son's wife didn't enter his mind. The fact that, if his son found out that he had tried to force himself on Miryam, he could legitimately *kill* him – *after he killed Miryam* - didn't enter his mind. What *did* enter his mind was that *Hasna knew.*

It was the season of harvesting the olives. For several days the entire village would be in the olive groves. They were armed with ladders upon which to climb in order to shake the olives from the upper branches of the trees; they had long sticks with which to beat olives from the lower branches so they would shower down onto the sheets spread beneath the trees. The olives weren't *picked* from the trees; they were *beaten* from the trees.

Women and children gathered the olives from the sheets, careful to exclude the leaves and bits of broken branch, into baskets. The full baskets were emptied into sacks to be carried back to the house where they would be piled until spread in the courtyard and left for three or four days to reduce the acidity of the eventual oil.

It was a festive time. People sang as they worked; people told stories; women unpacked picnic baskets of food for the workers and everyone ate; *accidents happened.*

Salma, Miryam, and Hasna spread the large sheet under the first tree. Awad had propped a ladder against the trunk. Saif and Ali had already scrambled up the ladder and were precariously balancing on the upper branches, when Abdallah turned to Hasna and said, "*Ya binit,* go up the ladder to that side of the tree," pointing to a sturdy branch that overhung a rocky outcrop.

She obeyed. She stepped out onto the sturdy limb; her calloused feet sought a sure footing; her toes curled around the smooth, slippery branch. She reached the branches above her and began to shake them. Like rain the olives showered about her.

Abdallah took a long stick and began to beat the branches. At first he beat the branches to the left of where Hasna was standing, and then he beat the branches to the right of where she was standing. The olives continued to fall from the branches that Saif and Ali were shaking, from the branches that Awad was hitting with his stick, from the shaking and beating of Hasna and Abdallah.

Salma and Miryam were busy gathering the olives into baskets; their heads were bent to their work. The neighbors were busy with their own trees, no one was watching Abdallah.

He took a mighty swing and the heavy stick cracked down on Hasna's bare toes. Her heart leapt into her throat as she grabbed the branches above her and felt her feet slip from the limb. The olive branches she grasped were weak and tender; she started to fall.

At last her scream got beyond the lump in her throat, her mother looked up in alarm; her little brothers started to scurry down the branches to reach her, calling, "Hasna! Hasna! Hold on!"

Salma pushed Abdallah aside and with her own body broke Hasna's fall. Mother and daughter lay there unmoving. Awad, Miryam, Saif and Ali gathered around the two women. Abdallah stood to the side. "*Yaba,* didn't you see her!" Awad asked, almost, accusingly.

"I didn't see her standing so close to the edge of the branch," Abdallah lied. "Is she alright?"

Hasna opened her blue eyes and stared into the concerned faces hovering above her. Salma also moved beneath her. Awad and Miryam lifted Hasna off her mother and bent to help Salma up.

Im Hussein, the midwife who had delivered all of Salma's nineteen babies, rushed over. She examined Salma. "I think her arm is dislocated," she said. She felt around the arm and socket. With Awad holding her steady, Im Hussein pushed the arm back into its socket. Salma groaned, but did not cry out.

"She will be fine in two or three days. She just needs to rest that arm," Im Hussein said. "How did Hasna fall?" she asked.

"Accidents happen," Abdallah said. "The girl is alright, isn't she?"

Im Hussein ran knowing hands over Hasna. There were no broken bones, only some scrapes, *illhumdillah*- praise God- on her arms and legs where she had been cut by the twigs as she fell.

Hasna dusted herself off and, looking defiantly at her father, gingerly climbed the ladder again. She climbed to the highest part of the tree; Saif and Ali climbed behind her and positioned themselves on either side of her. Once again the olives fell like rain.

Miryam helped Salma back to the house.

"That was no *accident*," Salma said grimly to herself.

"I know," was all that Miryam said.

In spite of her dislocated arm; in spite of his obsession with Miryam; in spite of his having attempting to murder his own daughter, Abdallah tried to mount Salma that night.

As he lay upon her, lifted her skirt and got into position, he felt the blade of a knife against his groin.

"I know you can kill me, but not *before I cut them off!*" Salma hissed.

Abdallah's hands encircled her neck. The blade of Salma's knife drew blood; he shriveled in fear. He realized *she meant it!*

He rolled off her and saw there was blood, *his blood,* spotting the pallet. It wasn't much blood; Salma had only scratched him, but it was *just enough.*

Salma silently got up and slipped under the blanket on the pallet where Hasna slept. It was the very first time in twelve years that Hasna could remember being held by her mother.

Nothing was ever said, but from that night Abdallah slept alone.

He threatened Salma. *"I will divorce you,"* he said.

She had responded. *"Divorce me and I will tell the imam, the sheikh, the mukhtar, your brothers, the neighbors – everyone – how you tried to kill Hasna! I will go to the coffeehouse and shout in the street how you tried to kill your daughter – perhaps I should add how you tried to rape your son's wife!"* Salma saw the astonished look of truth in Abdallah's face. She hadn't known about the attempted rape; she had *guessed* that Hasna had seen something she should not have seen.

Abdallah did not divorce her. He could not risk the shunning that would result from the words that Salma threatened to utter. They continued to live in the same house, but never again shared the same pallet. They moved silently, *resentfully,* around each other.

Abdallah sought a new wife – a young wife – a wife like Miryam. No one would give him. Some of the men *would* have given their daughters to Abdallah, but they hadn't counted on the stubborn unity of the women in the village. The women had agreed that none of their daughters would be given to Abu Issa; no matter how much money he offered; no matter how generous the gifts he promised.

It was a bit ironic; it was Abdallah's belief in his male superiority that had united the women.

Chapter 6

Abdallah became more taciturn and morose. He spent long hours at the coffeehouse. He spent long hours at the homes of his married children from his first wife. He chose to ignore the coolness with which his visits were greeted. It seemed the whole village *knew*, though it was never *said*, that he had purposely tried to kill his own daughter.

As winter approached, and the work in the fields and groves was done, Salma, Miryam, and Hasna wove baskets and trays from the straw that had been gleaned from the threshing. The unbroken, longer stalks were saved for the making of baskets.

The stalks were soaked in the *lagan* – the copper basin which was used for washing clothes – to make them flexible and easy to handle. Some of the shorter stalks were dyed: red, green, orange, or purple and used for decorating the weaving. While the women worked, the stalks were kept damp to keep them flexible.

Three straw stalks were braided together and twisted into a coil. Around this coil, other plaited stalks were added; they were held in place and bound to the previous coil with straw stems – some of which had been dyed. The women created a variety of functional and decorative objects. There were different kinds of *tabaq esh–* round trays of straw; large ones were made to use on the floor as a table upon which to spread the family meal; plain ones were made to use as lids to cover the wooden bowl in which dough was made or upon which to carry the baked bread from the *taboon;* some were used as decorative pieces to hang against the smooth, white surface of the *khabiyeh.*

Salma, Miryam and Hasna made round baskets – *juneh* for bread. They made round baskets called *qadah* for fruits. These baskets were covered with hide to protect the fruits from moisture.

Miryam was especially talented in basket weaving. She excelled in making *quteh* - small baskets shaped like a box and decorated with embroidery threads and fringe. In these, a woman could keep her trinkets, her scarves; the *kohl* for her eyes, embroidery thread, needles, scissors, the key to her bridal chest.

It was the making of a *quteh* that was the ultimate cause of Abdallah's downfall. Awad had gone to visit his older half-brothers. Salma and Hasna were weaving *tabaq esh* around the *kanun.* Saif and Ali had gone to play with Helweh and Henneh's children. Miryam, who had been sitting around the *kanun* with her mother-in-law and Hasna, went down to the *qa'albayt* to get the dyed straw she wanted to use in the *quteh* she was making.

It was relatively dark on the first floor. She opened the door so there would be some light as she searched for the colored straw she wanted. She had remembered placing it on a low shelf at the back. Luckily, she found it without much trouble. She turned to go back up the stone stairs when a hand clamped over her mouth and an arm grabbed her around the waist.

She was dragged back into a pile of straw and thrown down. Before she could scream, a knife was put at her throat pricking her *just a little.* Abdallah stared down at her frightened face. There was a look of madness about his eyes and in his grin. He fumbled with his *umbaz* as he raised her skirts above her waist. He ran a rough hand between her thighs, prying her legs apart. He fisted himself and was just ready to thrust into her, when he felt the wooden prongs of a pitchfork used in winnowing at his back.

He reared his head back and beheld the blue eyes, red hair, and freckles of Hasna. Behind her, another pitchfork in her hands stood Salma. Miryam pushed her skirts down around her ankles and pushed Abdallah off her. She was shaking and crying hysterically.

"Go upstairs, *binti,*" Salma said. Instead, Miryam, still crying hysterically, picked up the remaining wooden fork. Abdallah tried to move out of the circle of the three women. He couldn't.

It seemed the four of them were frozen in a bizarre tableau. Abdallah shouted; he ordered; he cursed. All his words fell on deaf ears.

Saif and Ali were the first to come home. They stood at the threshold speechless. There was their father surrounded by their mother, their sister, and their brother's wife – the three women threatening their father with pitchforks.

"Go fetch your brother, *Yum'ma,*" Salma said. "Tell him that I want him – *only that,* nothing more."

"What do you think you can do to *me?!*" Abdallah sneered.

"You will see what your *son* does! *We* are only keeping you here for him. What can *we* do? *We* are only women," Salma said sarcastically.

It wasn't long before Awad was there. He took in the scene: his mother, his sister, his crying wife, his father. He knew, without being told, what had happened.

"Miryam, are you hurt?" he asked, not taking his eyes off his father.

"*La,* Hasna and *Mart Ammie* got here just in time," she sobbed.

"The three of you go upstairs. Take Saif and Ali with you," he ordered. "*GO! NOW!*" he shouted.

The three women placed their wooden pitchforks near the door. Hasna took Saif and Ali's hands and pulled them up the stone stairs.

They heard shouts and shuffling. They did not go down the stairs. They heard the outside door slammed shut and the rusty bolt slid across barring entrance. Still they did not go down the stone stairs. There was more shuffling, and then there was silence.

Awad came slowly up the stairs. A bruise was forming under his left eye; his lips were bloody; there were angry tears in his eyes. "Father has had a heart attack, I think, *Allah yer'hum'o*- God have mercy on him."

He sat next to the *kanun*, put his head in his arms and wept. Miryam went over and rested her hand on his shoulder; he angrily brushed it off.

Salma, Hasna and the boys went down to the lower level. They pushed the rusty bolt back so the door could be opened to let in some light. Abdallah lay across the straw. His eyes were open, but he saw nothing.

Salma went over and closed the lids over his eyes. Hasna and the boys had already started to rake and straighten the straw-strewn floor.

"Go and bring in the sheep and goats," Hasna said to her little brothers.

Awad came down the stairs. His face was wet with tears. He picked up his father's arms; Salma and Hasna took his feet. Out from beneath his worn *umbaz*, the black snake slithered.

They carried him upstairs and laid him on a pallet. Salma washed him, her hands recoiling when she touched his flesh.

"You need to go and call Im Hussein, *Yum'ma,*" Salma said to Awad. "Tell her there has been a death in the family. You must go and call your half-brothers as well. You must tell them that their father has had a heart attack."

Salma, Hasna, Miryam, Saif and Ali sat in a circle around Abdallah's body.

"You are each to forget what happened here this evening, *Yum'ma,*" Salma said. "Your father, May *Allah* forgive him, had a bad heart which finally gave out. It *was written* that he would die this day. This is the *will of Allah.*"

They each nodded. The secret of what had happened that night would *never* be voiced, not even among them. In their hearts they *knew* Abdallah had not died of a heart attack. He had been killed by Awad, his *son.* It had been an *honor killing,* a killing they felt that even God Himself would approve.

Chapter 7

A difficult and painful death was the punishment for sins committed on earth; that was what Islam taught. There was *no* doubt in Awad's, or Salma's, or Hasna's, or Miryam's mind that Abdallah had gotten the death *he had earned.*

"You must live good lives to have a good death," Salma had told Saif and Ali. Even *they* understood that their father had not been a good man.

Abdallah's two older sons came and took charge of the funeral preparations. His body was wrapped in a burial shroud. The door was taken off its hinges and balanced on four rocks, two at each end; Abdallah's wrapped body was placed upon the door. The body would lie on the board in the upper room until the next morning when he would be buried.

All night women from the family kept vigil over the body. Kerosene lamps were lit so the mourners were not in complete darkness. In the courtyard, the men from the family kept their own vigil by moonlight. There was a full moon, just like there had been the night that Hasna was born.

Only women from the immediate family kept vigil that night: Helweh, Henneh, and Abdallah's two daughters from his first marriage; his older sons' wives, the wives of Abdallah's brothers, and of course Salma, Hasna and Miryam.

There was *no* tearing of clothing; *no* beating of breasts; *no* scratching and slapping of faces; *no* hands or faces blackened with soot; there was *no* violent emotion *as custom dictated.* All of the women present *knew* what Abdallah had been like. Tomorrow, when the neighbor women came, perhaps his daughters from his first marriage, and the wives of his older sons, *would* cry and slap their faces and beat their breasts to *show* their *pretended* grief. If they didn't, the neighbor women would gossip. Salma was an *outsider,* even though she had lived in the village for almost twenty years, and she didn't *care* what the neighbor women thought.

The afternoon of the funeral, Abdallah's body was carried to the cemetery on the door. Abdallah's friends from the coffeehouse, the neighbor men, and his sons accompanied the body to the grave, even Saif and Ali walked in the procession. The women followed discreetly from a distance.

At the gravesite, the Imam asked if anyone would like to bear witness to Abdallah's good deeds. His question was met with silence. Everyone *knew* that Abdallah had been a sinful man. The Imam prayed that Abdallah would find forgiveness and absolution in the next life.

Before Abdallah's body was lowered into the hole, Salma stepped forward and climbed into the grave!

"I request that I and my children be allowed to remain in my husband's house for the duration of our lives. I do not wish to return to my village and the house of my father." She looked directly at Abdallah's older sons who had a claim to their father's house. A request from the grave, in the presence of the Imam and the men from the village, could not be ignored. The burial would not be allowed to take place unless the request was granted.

"*Mart Abou'ee* (Father's wife)" Abdallah's oldest son answered. "You and your children, of course, must live out the duration of your lives in our father's house. This is *our* wish." He reached down a hand and helped his father's wife out of the grave.

Abdallah was lowered into the narrow grave. His oldest son positioned the body on its side with the right hand under the head. Dirt was sprinkled over the shroud as his son said, "*This is thy share of the world.*"

The village men standing around the grave were curious about the body's condition. If the hands were soft, and not rigid, this would mean that the deceased was a generous man. If the body was still yellow, and had not begun to turn black, this would mean that the deceased had lived a good life. When the winding sheet was removed from around Abdallah's face, tinges of black could be seen around his nostrils and lips; when his oldest son positioned his father's right hand beneath his head, it had been difficult to bend as it had become quite rigid.

The ritual meals were prepared and served to the mourners; the forty days of mourning were observed; custom was followed as though Abdallah had been a good man.

For forty days Awad refrained from any intimacy with Miryam. Part of him *blamed* her for his father's death. *If she hadn't flirted with his father, he would be alive,* he thought. *If she hadn't led him on, he would be alive. It was expected that a man would give in to temptation, especially if there was a temptress like Miryam.*

Miryam had *missed another period.* In six years she had only been pregnant once. Her periods had always been regular, and now she *suspected* – she *knew* – she was with child. The knowledge terrified her. It was a *punishment* from God. That night she hesitantly told Awad, "Awad, I am with child."

He rolled over and looked at her.

"With child? Are you sure?"

Miryam nodded her head. "Are you pleased?" she said hopefully.

He turned away from her and rolled onto his side. Miryam lay on her back and silently cried as she stared into the darkness.

Awad lay awake for some time; he, too, stared into the darkness and wondered, *Is this child mine, or my father's? He wondered if Miryam had told him everything that had happened before Hasna came into the qa'albayt.*

Miryam's pregnancy was nothing like the first one. She was lethargic; she gained a lot of weight; her hair lost its luster; her legs and feet were swollen; and she felt nauseous most of the time. Miryam *knew* this was God's retribution for what had happened in the *qa'albayt.*

"I don't understand, *binti,* how you have put on so much weight when you hardly keep anything down," Salma said.

Hasna started doing Miryam's chores without being asked.

"You, rest, *okht'ee- my sister,* I'll do your chores," Hasna had said. There had sprung up between Miryam and Hasna an *understanding* that *bordered* on friendship. Hasna would bring her tea; Hasna would help her up off the pallet; Hasna would carry little Abdallah around so Miryam would not be bothered with a demanding toddler.

The day before Hasna turned thirteen, Miryam went into labor.

Salma sent for Im Hussein; Awad went to the coffeehouse; Saif and Ali took little Abdallah to spend the day with Helweh and her children.

Miryam's labor was nothing like that she had had with little Abdallah. The pains were strong and close together, yet the baby had not dropped. Salma and Hasna walked her around the room; she clutched their hands as a pain rent her body; the midwife examined her again and again. Still the baby had not dropped into position.

Im Hussein whispered to Salma, "Something is terribly wrong; the baby should have descended into the birth canal by now. I don't like this at all."

Im Hussein had Miryam lay on a carpet, and she, along with Hasna and Salma, *rolled* Miryam from side to side, hoping to *loosen* the baby.

Im Hussein told Salma, "Send Hasna for Helweh. She shouldn't be here; she is too young to see this. She can stay with Helweh's children while Helweh comes to help."

Hasna was *glad* to go. What *was* happening to Miryam scared her. *"If this is what happens,"* she thought, *"I am glad I have red hair, blue eyes and freckles and that no one would want me!"*

Finally after six hours of extreme labor, the baby dropped. Im Hussein looked; the door of the womb had opened. She looked to see if the baby had presented his head, what she saw was a *foot!*

She grimly looked at Salma and Helweh and shook her head. "I'm afraid the baby is coming feet-first."

Salma massaged Miryam's extended belly; Miryam clutched Helweh's hands as she writhed on the pallet and muttered prayers to Allah to help her, though deep inside she knew He wouldn't. "I'm going to die! I'm going to die!" she moaned.

Im Hussein reached up a gnarled hand and gently pulled out two little feet. "Don't push, *binti, don't push!"*

Miryam panted and tried *not* to push. She clutched Helweh's hands in an iron grip, as though if she held on strong enough, Helweh would keep her from slipping into hell.

Im Hussein gently tried to pull out the two little legs. "Very gently, *binti,* one very small push."

Miryam strained just a little – the pain was incredible. The legs would *not* descend. Im Hussein reached up. The legs seemed tight against the baby's chest. She couldn't pry them loose. She tugged; they wouldn't budge.

Miryam was exhausted; her breathing was shallow; her grip on Helweh's hands was lax. Miryam looked over at her mother-in-law and whispered, trying to tell her something. Her lips moved but no words came out.

Salma put her ear against Miryam's mouth and felt the words of confession.

Miryam gave a deep sigh as the spirit rushed out of her body.

Im Hussein took a knife out of her sash and slashed the door to the womb open. She worked frantically as she ripped through the wound and extracted the infant.

The infant was almost black in color and quite shriveled. It looked like a very old man. The cord was around the neck like a strangling noose.

"It has been dead a long time," Im Hussein said. There were tears in her eyes. She placed the shriveled, blackened corpse on a straw tray and threw a rag over it.

Salma raised the closed lids and looked into Miryam's sightless eyes. She gently closed the lids; the thick, dark lashes fanned out against Miryam's pale cheek. Salma resignedly sighed.

"She is gone, and the infant is gone, *Allah yer'hum'hom-may God's mercy be upon them.*" As she wiped Miryam's brow, she said to herself: "It is for the best." In her heart she cursed Abdallah and prayed that he was burning in hell.

Forty days after the death of Miryam and her son, Awad married Sabha, a girl of fourteen. Not surprisingly, she was very much like Miryam – she even resembled her in that she was buxom and pretty; had long raven braids that reached below her knees; had a face without blemish, and outlined her dark eyes with *kohl*. And like Miryam, at least Miryam in the beginning, she thought that the red-haired, blue-eyed, freckled Hasna was about the ugliest girl she had ever seen.

Chapter 8

Little Abdallah clung to Hasna and wanted nothing to do with his father's new wife. That suited Sabha just fine! *After all, Abdallah isn't my child,* she said to herself. At meal times, Abdallah sat in Hasna's lap; at night he slept with Hasna; it was Hasna who dressed him, gave him his weekly bath, and carried him around when he was irritable and tired. Just as Saif and Ali adored Hasna, little Abdallah did, too.

His father's wife would scold him; his father's wife would box his ears when no one was looking; his father's wife pinched him if he cried; it was so *obvious* that she didn't like him. Hasna, on the other hand, was always patient and kind and loving.

Sabha had once overheard Salma talking to Hasna.

"I don't know how I will ever find you a husband, *Yum'ma.* You work hard, you are good-natured, but with *red hair, blue eyes, and freckles* no man is going to want you." Hasna didn't *mind;* after what she has seen of childbirth, she was *glad* that no man would want a red haired, blue-eyed wife with freckles.

"Perhaps if he is *blind, Mart Ammie,*" Sabha had laughed. "Perhaps an old man with poor eyesight will want her as a third wife!" she chuckled.

"This is none of your business, *kintee* (daughter-in-law)" Salma answered sharply. "There is *no one* who works as hard, and as willingly, as good-naturedly, as Hasna. She can't help the way she was born. This is the will of Allah."

Sabha tossed her raven braids, moistened her red lips, and flashed her eyes outlined in *kohl.* "I meant nothing by it, *Mart Ammie.* I was just *joking,"* Sabha replied. Salma knew it wasn't a joke, and so did Hasna.

Like Miryam before her, Sabha spent a great deal of time in front of the little fringed mirror that hung from the embroidered pouch that contained her bottle of *kohl.* She was pleased with her beautiful reflection. Once when Hasna was passing with Abdallah in her arms, Sabha covered the mirror with her hands.

"Don't ever look in my mirror, Hasna! Your face will break it," she laughed. "Mirrors are only for pretty faces, not for a face like yours!"

Hasna repositioned Abdallah on her hip and didn't say anything. *They're only words,* she thought, *but it would have been nice to be pretty enough to want a mirror.*

Hasna was resigned to the way she looked. She wasn't a faded, though pretty, print of her mother like Helweh and Henneh were. She wasn't buxom and comely like Sabha was. She was skinny and flat-chested. There was no point in *wishing* she was pretty, she *wasn't.* She half-believed that what Sabha had so flippantly said was true: *The only man who would want her would be blind, old, or both.*

None of her aunts wanted her for their sons. She had overheard her mother talking to her aunts, or rather her aunts talking to her mother.

"Hasna is a hard worker; Hasna is easy-going; Hasna is so good with Saif and Ali and little Abdallah; she will make a wonderful mother, but..."

There was always a 'but', Hasna thought. Her aunts always said the same words after the 'but', "but she's not very pretty."

When a man took a wife to bed, he *didn't* care if she could make baskets, weave rugs, make clay pots, pick olives, wash dishes, lug pallets out to the sun, or carry water from the well in an earthenware jug on her head. He *didn't* care – at least then – if she was a good cook; could milk the goats and make cheese and yogurt. A man, when he took a wife to bed, wanted someone who was soft, round, willing, and *pretty* – even *if he wouldn't be able to see in the dark if she had red hair, blue eyes, and freckles.*

Like her mother, Hasna, too, despaired that she would ever be married. *Not* that she *wanted* to be married, but it was unfortunately true that an unmarried girl had no status, no definition. She was merely a daughter in her father's house, or in her case, *in her brother's house.* If she remained unmarried, she would be little more than a servant to her brother's wife – to Sabha.

Im Mansur came to visit Salma unexpectedly.

Salma knew Im Mansur only casually. The village was small; everyone was acquainted, but one tended to only *socialize* within the family – the clan.

They sat out in the sun of the courtyard. They made small talk before Im Mansur finally got to the purpose of her visit.

"As you know, Im Issa, my oldest son, Mansur, is now eighteen. It is time he settled down and took a wife. I have suggested a number of his cousins to him, but he is quite adamant; he has a *particular* girl in mind."

"Who is she?" Salma asked.

"No, he hasn't actually *seen* the girl. He told me that he has only *seen* her in his dreams," Im Mansur shook her head and smiled sheepishly.

"I asked him to describe her to me. He said that the girl in his dreams has: *red hair, blue eyes, and freckles.*"

Salma was puzzled, and just a little astonished. "Why, you have described my daughter, Hasna!"

"Yes, that is what I thought, too. Of course, I have seen Hasna from a distance when she picked olives, or took her younger brothers out, or when she went to the well. I even remember you carrying her on your shoulder when she was just a little thing. One couldn't *miss* that flaming red hair!"

Salma spoke bluntly. "Hasna *is* a hard worker; she *is* easy-going; she *is* good with her younger brothers and her nephew, Abdallah, but *she is not pretty.*"

Im Mansur was also blunt. "I know she is not pretty, at least in the way that most people judge beauty. I have told my son that he should marry one of his cousins, or a girl from the clan, who is dark and beautiful. He is quite adamant that he will have no one but a red haired, blue-eyed girl with freckles."

"Are you *asking* for Hasna?" Salma questioned. "She is only thirteen and a half."

"Yes, I would like for you to ask Hasna if she would consider marrying Mansur. I realize that Abu Mansur must officially speak to your son and Hasna's uncles, but I wanted to sound out you and Hasna first."

"We must drink coffee," Salma said. "Hasna! Hasna! Bring the coffee, *Yum'ma,*" Salma called.

Hasna had covered her hair and braids with a long, once-white shawl. She carried the tray of coffee out and offered coffee first to Im Mansur and then to her mother. Little Abdallah was holding securely to her skirt and sucking his thumb.

She kept her eyes down as she smiled and said to Im Mansur, "Abdallah is never beyond arm's reach of my skirt. He thinks I am his mother," she laughed.

She put the tray, with a long handled pot of coffee on it, down on a thresh-bottomed stool. Not the least bit self-consciously, she picked up the toddler and blew bubbles in his neck. "You have seen the guest, you naughty boy, *now* we have work to do," she laughed as she carried him into the house.

It hadn't entered her mind that Im Mansur had come to *look at her.*

Im Mansur thoughtfully drank her coffee. When Salma asked her if she would like another cup, she absently said she would.

"This is very good coffee," she remarked.

"Hasna made it," Salma answered.

As Im Mansur got up to go, she kissed Im Issa on both cheeks. "Please talk over with Hasna what we have discussed. I will come back in two or three days to get your answer."

When Salma went inside, Hasna had just put Abdallah down for a nap. Sabha was sitting on the floor picking through the lentils that would be cooked for dinner.

"What did your visitor want, *Mart Ammie?*" Sabha asked.

"She is interested in Hasna for her son," Salma said, still somewhat, unbelieving.

"*Hasna?!* Is he *blind?*" Sabha asked in astonishment.

"No, he is *not* blind," Salma sharply said. "But I think he might be a little *slow,*" she half-said to herself.

Chapter 9

Mansur was pacing the courtyard when his mother got back. "What did they say, *Yum'ma?*" he asked.

"Give me time to catch my breath, *Yum'ma,* don't be so impatient!"

"What did they say, *habeeptee, Yum'ma?*" Mansur coaxed.

"Im Issa said that she would talk to her daughter, talk to her son, and that I should come back in two or three days for her answer."

"Did you *see* the girl, *Yum'ma?*"

"I saw her. She is like you described. She has red hair, blue eyes, and freckles." Im Mansur paused, "She is *not* very pretty. I *do* wish you would let me go and talk to your uncles. There are several girls among your cousins who are beautiful. I'm sure any one of them would be *perfect* for you."

Mansur was not convinced; he stubbornly held to the vision he had been given.

"What is she like, *Yum'ma?*"

"Like? How do I know what she is *like?* Her mother says she is hard working, and kind; she says that her daughter smiles a lot and is good with her younger brothers and her toddler nephew. In fact, when the girl served the coffee, her little nephew was hanging onto her skirt. She even joked with me that the little one was never beyond the reach of her skirt – that, in fact, he probably thought that she was his mother!"

"What is her name, *Yum'ma?*"

"She is called *Hasna."*

"*Hasna,"* Mansur said savoring the name. It meant *one who is beautiful!*

Salma talked candidly with Hasna.

"You probably will *not* get another offer, *Yum'ma,"* Salma said. "If you do, it will be from an old man who is a widower, or one who wants a second wife, or someone who wants a girl to take care of him." Salma paused. "You are *not* pretty," she said bluntly.

"Im Mansur's son is only eighteen. His age is certainly in his favor."

"Is there something *wrong* with him, *Yum'ma?*"

"Wrong? No, I don't think there is anything *wrong.* He might be a bit *slow,"* Salma added.

"A man would have to be a *bit slow,* wouldn't he; to want a girl who looks like me?" Hasna added, angry at herself for the tears that stung her eyes.

Salma *was* sympathetic to Hasna's pain, or at least she *wanted* to be, but life had taught her that it was better to *face reality* rather than to pretend it was different than what it really was.

"I think you must accept this offer, *Yum'ma*. I will talk to Awad and your uncles, but they will not object."

That night as Hasna pulled the covers over Saif and Ali and Abdallah, Saif put his hands on Hasna's cheeks and asked, "Are you going to leave us, Hasna? *Mart Abou'ee* (father's wife) says you are going to leave us."

Hasna glanced over at Sabha. "Perhaps I will be moving to another house, *habeebee,* but I will always come and visit you, and you will always come and visit me. And you know," she said, placing his hand against her heart, "you, and Ali, and Abdallah always live *right here in my heart.* That will *never change."*

She bent down and kissed him on the cheek. She reached over and kissed Ali, who had already puckered up for *his* kiss. She lay down beside the sleeping Abdallah and drew him into her arms. *How can I ever leave him?* She thought.

No one had objected! Hasna had *wished* that they hadn't been quite so *relieved* though! *"You could almost hear a collective sigh,"* she thought. She could almost hear their thoughts, *"Thank God, someone asked for Hasna. And he isn't old; and he isn't blind! It's a miracle!"*

Im Mansur, once she had received a positive answer from Salma, had sent her husband, his brothers, and

Mansur to formally ask for Hasna's hand from her brother and uncles. Hasna was not present.

The next day the Imam from the mosque came and sat with Hasna and Salma. He asked Hasna if she was *being pressured* in any way. Hasna said that she had not been pressured, that she was agreeing to marry of her own free will.

The marriage contract was drawn up and signed. Mansur and Hasna had not, as yet, even seen each other. Awad had signed as a witness. Hasna had made her "X"; she could neither read nor write. Mansur and his father signed in the presence of Awad. The *fatiha-* the opening verse from the Koran was read; Mansur and Hasna were legally married.

Im Mansur and Im Issa, along with their sisters-in-law, had taken the bus to Bethlehem to buy gold and a trousseau. Hasna did not go along. It was as though she was not a participant in her wedding, but a doll to be dressed and adorned and presented to the groom the night of the wedding as a gift to unwrap.

Rather than buy a new bridal chest, Salma had given Hasna the bridal chest that had been Miryam's. In it Hasna placed her everyday shifts, the new clothes that Im Mansur had bought, two of the baskets she had made, and an embroidered pillow sham that she had made one winter. In the bottom of the chest, she found Miryam's mirror. She looked at her reflection and sighed. *"I'm really **not** very pretty,"* she said to herself.

She carefully wrapped the mirror in a kerchief and replaced it in the bottom of the chest beneath the worn shifts.

It had finally occurred to Sabha that once Hasna was gone, *she, Sabha,* would have to work! All the work that Hasna had done, Sabha would be expected to do. She would no longer be *pampered* as the new bride; she would have to accept responsibility for Abdallah; she would become a *slave* to her mother-in-law; literally -the honeymoon was over. She had been *so sure* that Hasna would never marry; that no one in their right mind would ask for a girl with red hair, blue eyes and freckles!

Hasna was worried about Abdallah. He had lost his mother; his father's wife didn't like him; and now he was going to lose *her.* She *wished* there was some way that she could take Abdallah with her. She *knew* it was impossible. Awad would never agree to let his son live with strangers; her new mother-in-law, and the husband she hadn't seen, would never agree to her bringing with her a child – even *if* Awad agreed.

Every night when she kissed Saif and Ali good-night she would say to them, "I'm counting on you two to look out for Abdallah. He is so small, and he will need two big brothers like you to watch out for him. Promise me that you will take extra special care of him."

"We promise, Hasna, we will."

Just by chance, the next afternoon, Im Mansur stopped in. Hasna was sitting in the courtyard enjoying the sun, cradling Abdallah in her lap. He was contentedly sucking his thumb as he patted Hasna's face. He looked adoringly at her and would smile around his thumb.

As Im Mansur visited with Salma, she kept looking over at Hasna and Abdallah.

"The child is going to miss, Hasna. How old is he?" Im Mansur asked.

"He has just turned two. And, yes, he *will* miss Hasna. Since his mother died, Hasna has had the complete care of him." Salma sighed, "And Hasna will miss him!"

"Hasn't your son remarried?"

"Yes, his wife is young, and as yet, has no children of her own. She finds it hard to feel *motherly* toward Abdallah. She will in time." Salma added. "Once Hasna leaves us, Sabha *will* have to take responsibility for Abdallah."

Im Mansur again glanced over at Hasna. Hasna was kissing Abdallah's curls and tickling him under his chin. If Im Mansur was anything, she was *maternal*. She felt for the child, Abdallah, and she felt for the child, Hasna.

"I know it is very unusual," Im Mansur began, "but do you think that your son would allow Abdallah to come with Hasna for a short while – just to ease the transition for the baby and for her? After all, we are now *na'sigh'ib*- related by marriage," she added.

"Awad would *never* agree, nor do I suspect your husband and son would agree," Salma replied, somewhat astonished by the request.

"It would only be for a very little while. Please ask him. I hate to think of separating those two," she said glancing again at the tableau of *mother-and-child*.

Salma *did* ask Awad in the presence of Sabha. Her ears perked right up, and her dark eyes brightened. She waited to hear what Awad would say.

"It is out of the question, *Yum'ma*. My son stays here – he has a new mother now," he said looking meaningfully at Sabha.

"It would only be for a little while, until Abdallah is *weaned* from Hasna and Hasna from him. Soon he will be going with Saif and Ali to herd the sheep and goats. Soon he will be playing with the boys in the *hara*- the neighborhood and will no longer need a mother's lap in which to sit." Salma knew full well how Sabha felt about Abdallah; she didn't want Abdallah put in Sabha's care, but the final word was not hers; it was Awad's.

"*My son stays here!*" Awad said adamantly.

"Sabha is young and as yet has no children of her own. It is hard for her to feel *motherly* toward Abdallah." Salma argued. "Abdallah is *attached* to Hasna and almost looks at her as being his mother."

"*Mart Ammie* is right husband," Sabha interjected. "Abdallah, *habeebee,* is very attached to Hasna. Perhaps *he needs this transition.*" Sabha hoped she sounded convincing and not *too eager.*

"Her new husband will not want a wife *with a child in tow,*" Awad argued. Both Salma and Sabha could tell that he was weakening.

"I said the very thing to Im Mansur. She assured me that now that we are *na'sigh'ib* it was no problem. The *suggestion* did come from her."

"What will the people in the village say if I allow my son to go and live in another man's house?"

"The village is small. They *all* know how attached Hasna and Abdallah are. Though it *is* unusual, they would probably think that it was a kind and generous thing that both you and Hasna's new family were doing. After all, it would only be for a little while."

"Let me think about it. I want to also talk with Hasna's new in-laws before I decide."

That night, after Awad had rolled off Sabha, she stroked his sweaty chest and said, "It would be cruel to Abdallah to lose Hasna when he is still so little. Think of what would be best for Abdallah, *habeebee.* It would *only* be for a little while. When you think about it, *it is really a very good plan.*"

"You really think so?" Awad said kissing her. He felt himself once more aroused, and as he rolled on top of her thought: *perhaps it is a very good plan.*

Chapter 10

The only instructions that Salma gave Hasna the day of her wedding was: *lay back, don't cry, and thank God that someone married you.* Hasna was convinced that the only thing going for Mansur was that he was eighteen! She *knew* he must be short with weak eyes, and was probably *slow;* why else would he want someone with red hair, blue eyes and freckles? (Hasna had no way of knowing that in the Scottish glen of her Crusader ancestor, she would have been considered a *beauty!*)

Salma had insisted that Hasna be covered in *three* thick veils; *there is no point in flaunting her plainness,* she thought. Hasna could hardly *see* through the clouds of gauze. The point was *no one could see her.*

The wedding seemed to go on *around* her. She moved through a fog of gauze which not only hid her face but veiled her fear. She *heard* the singing, clapping, and ululations of the women. She *heard* the stamping feet of the men as they danced in front of her new home. She *felt* her mother-in-law pass her a piece of dough and instruct her to press it against the lintel of the door. She *felt* the hand of her mother on her arm as she ushered her into the bridal chamber. She *heard* the muffed voice of her mother through the veils' thickness repeat the same litany: *lay back, don't cry, and thank God that you are married.* She heard the door close, and *felt* alone and scared. She was only thirteen and a half – a *child*. She had been married off to a short, slow-witted, weak-eyed boy she had never *seen*.

She *knew* that when her bridegroom lifted her veils with the tip of his sword, he would be disappointed. He *may* have *dreamt* of a red-haired, blue-eyed girl with freckles, but a *dream* and *reality* were very different things. He would remove the veils and see a short, freckled, flat-chested child with red hair who was made-up to look like a bride.

Hasna heard the door open and close. She heard footsteps approach her. She could barely see through the veils she wore the shape of a man with a sword in his hand.

With the tip of his sword, Mansur lifted the veils one by one. As each veil was lifted, Hasna's vision of her husband became clearer. When the last veil had been lifted and she could clearly *see* Mansur, the quick tongue that accompanied the red hair found voice.

Mansur was tall and strong. He had flashing dark eyes, black curly hair, and a ready smile.

"Why, you aren't short, or weak-sighted, or *slow!* You are the handsomest man I have ever seen! Why, on earth, would you have wanted to marry someone like me?!" Hasna sobbed.

"Hasna, stop crying! *Hasna, STOP CRYING!"* Mansur rubbed the tears from her cheeks. The *kohl* outlining her blue eyes had made muddy trails down her cheeks.

He smiled at her. "I dreamt of a girl with red hair, blue eyes, and freckles. *You are nothing like my dream.*"

Hasna *knew* he would be disappointed! She *wished* she could have been pretty *for him*. She couldn't control the tears that flowed. *Of course she was nothing like his dream – she was ugly!*

"*You* are nothing like my dream, Hasna. *You* are more *beautiful* than I imagined you would be. You are a *Hourieh* fit for the Prophet himself."

Mansur was gentle and considerate. He *wooed* Hasna. He whispered in her ear how beautiful she was; how happy she made him; how fortunate he was that she had agreed to be his wife.

When it was over, he kissed her and smiled, "Now, we are truly one."

She dozed in the circle of his arms. She had *not imagined* that it would be like this. For the first time in her thirteen and a half years, she was *unbelievably happy!*

The next morning, as custom dictated, she went to the village well to fetch water. When Im Mansur looked at her that morning, she had to take a second look. *"Why, she is really quite lovely,"* she thought. *"There is a prettiness there that I didn't see before."*

One of the first guests to arrive to congratulate the newlyweds was Salma with Saif, Ali, and Abdallah. Salma looked keenly at her daughter to get a sense of how the *deflowering* had gone. There were *no* dark circles under Hasna's eyes; there were *no* unshed tears in frightened eyes; Hasna's smile did not seem as though it were forced.

Salma looked at her new son-in-law. He didn't *look* disappointed, distracted, bored. His smile seemed genuine; his eyes almost *danced* when they lighted on Hasna.

As soon as Abdallah saw Hasna, he wiggled out of his grandmother's arms and flung himself into Hasna's lap. He held tightly to her skirt and buried his face in her lap – breathing in her scent.

Hasna picked him up and kissed his fat cheeks. Abdallah would put his head down on her shoulder, and then raise it again, pat her cheeks and smile before snuggling once again against her neck.

Mansur reached over and ran a finger over Abdallah's fist. Abdallah shyly looked at him and tentatively smiled.

"You are going to stay with us for a while, *Ammo,"* Mansur said to Abdallah.

Hasna looked gratefully at Mansur. It had been agreed, after Awad had talked with Mansur and his parents, that Abdallah *would* be allowed to stay with Hasna for a short period of time – a *transitional period only,* Awad had stressed.

Saif and Ali went up and kissed and hugged Hasna. Mansur also kissed and hugged them.

"We are brothers-in-law now," he joked with the little boys. "You must come *every day* to see me and your sister. You must *promise!*"

"We promise," Saif and Ali said in chorus.

Mansur picked each one up and set them on his knees.

Salma looked at Hasna and Mansur with the children sitting in their laps, and she thought, *"Allah has written these two together. Mansur is perfect for Hasna and I believe that she is perfect for him. They are like two children 'playing house.'"*

When Awad and Sabha came to congratulate the newlyweds, Sabha almost had to physically close her mouth. She couldn't get over how truly *handsome* Mansur was, and she secretly wished that his mother had *asked for her!* Sabha was astonished when she looked at Hasna, *"She is almost pretty,"* she thought. *"She never looked like this at home!"*

That night when Mansur and Hasna retired to their room, Hasna carried a sleeping Abdallah in her arms. She was touched to see that Im Mansur had spread a small pallet next to the one that Hasna and Mansur shared.

She knelt down to place the sleeping Abdallah on his bed. Mansur knelt beside her and took the sleeping toddler from her arms. He laid him on the pallet and covered him. As he kissed him on the brow he whispered to Abdallah, "Sleep well, *Ammo.* Sleep well, *habeebee.*"

When Mansur had settled himself on top of Hasna, she wrapped her arms across his back and whispered into his ear, "Thank you for allowing Abdallah to stay with us. It would have broken my heart to have been separated from him when he is so little. Thank you for understanding."

Mansur smiled down at her. Thick black curls dusted his forehead. He kissed her nose and said, "How could I possibly separate a *mother* from her child – even a mother who is only thirteen and a half and still a bride!" he chuckled. "One day, *inshallah,* you will bear our sons, whom you will love as much as you love Abdallah. I am blessed to have a bride who loves children. *Inshallah* we will have many sons."

Before the month was out, Hasna had *swallowed a fly.* She was pleased that those nights of lying in Mansur's arms had borne fruit. He was *over the moon* when she whispered to him that she was *with child.*

The next day when she had taken Abdallah over to visit her family, she told her mother.

"You will be like me and your sisters," Salma said. "We all became pregnant easily; we all had *honeymoon* babies. Unlike Sabha," Salma whispered, "she still is not pregnant."

Awad had gotten used to Abdallah staying with Hasna. He had to admit to himself that his son was happy, probably happier than he would have been if he had been under the care of Sabha.

"When you are tired of Abdallah, you must bring him home," Awad would tell Hasna.

"*Do* let him stay a bit longer with us. He is no bother at all. He is *still* so little, and selfishly, I can't bear to be without him."

"There is not a *selfish* bone in your body, Hasna," Awad smiled. "I can *see* how happy and well Abdallah is. He may stay a little longer."

Sabha was both *glad* and *jealous*. She was glad that Abdallah would not be staying with them and that she would not have the responsibility of him, but she was *jealous* that Abdallah seemed to be doing so well with Hasna. She was also *jealous* and puzzled why Hasna had already *swallowed a fly,* and *she* had not.

Awad had fathered *two* children, so the problem was not with him; she feared the problem might be with *her*. If she did not give him children, he could legitimately put her aside and marry another.

She did not know that Awad had been married to Miryam *six years* before she conceived, and that Miryam's second child was probably not his.

Awad *also* worried about the fact that Sabha had not conceived. He *certainly* worked at it! He would have *liked* to have blamed her, but he remembered how difficult it had been for Miryam to conceive – at least the first time. His father had gotten his mother pregnant every year for nineteen years. His half-brothers both had large families. He secretly worried that the problem might lie with him.

He had taken to drinking a glass of olive oil every morning. He had been at the coffeehouse when a man was talking about his grandfather who was a *hundred-and-two* years old and had married a young woman of thirty. The men were joking with the man that his *grandfather probably no longer had a "stick."* The man had joked back that not only did his grandfather have a "*stick,*" but that his new wife was pregnant!

When asked how that was possible, the man had said, *"Every morning my grandfather drinks a glass of olive oil. He swears that it not only makes his 'stick' a 'club,' but that it makes him potent as well."*

Awad was *not* the only man, who hearing the story, had started to drink a glass of olive oil every morning!

Chapter 11

In the sixth months they had been married, Mansur had only *scolded* her once. Hasna was six months pregnant when he caught her at the top of the fig tree picking figs! She was tossing figs down to Abdallah who was trying to catch them in a basket. Both of them were laughing at the game.

Mansur *was not amused. "Sometimes Hasna **is** a child!"* he thought.

"*Hasna*, what do you think you are doing! Get down from there at once!" he commanded.

She adeptly worked her way down from branch-to-branch, pausing when she spied a plump, firm fig to toss down to Abdallah.

Mansur was frowning so that his bushy eyebrows almost met. Abdallah looked up at him and started to frown as well. He slipped his little hand into Mansur's hand and said, "*Hasna naughty.*" Mansur looked down at the frowning toddler and found it hard to keep his smile from twitching.

"*Muz'boot,* that's right, Hasna is naughty," he said squeezing Abdallah's hand.

When Hasna's bare feet finally hit the ground, she looked mischievously through twinkling blue eyes at Mansur. She wasn't the *least* repentant.

"Look at all the figs I picked," she beamed. "Abdallah was such a good boy to help me," she said running a hand through his curls.

"And *what* if you had fallen?" Mansur frowned. "What would have happened to the son that you carry then?"

"I had no intention of falling, besides *your son* enjoyed the exercise," she laughed.

Mansur bent down and spoke to Abdallah. "*Habeebee,* go and ask *Im'me* for a feather. Your *Amto Hasna* needs to be *beaten,*" he smiled.

"I *deserve* to be beaten, do I?"

"Wives who disobey their husbands and behave foolishly *must be beaten,*" Mansur said. "It says so in the Quran: '*if a wife disobeys, beat her with a feather to show her who is Master*'. I am just doing my husbandly duty."

It is hard to look masterful and husbandly when one is only eighteen, and one's wife is only fourteen. Abdallah dutifully returned with a feather that Im Mansur had plucked from the tail of the rooster. He handed it solemnly to Mansur.

Mansur took the feather and twirled it between his thumb and first finger. "Prepare to be beaten, Hasna," he said as his dark eyes snapped, and his lips twitched.

She turned her palm up and stretched her hand out to him. He swatted her open palm five times with the feather; he then raised her palm to his lips and kissed it.

"There, you must always obey me and *never* be foolish enough to climb to the top of a fig tree when you are six-months pregnant!"

Mansur bent down and picked up Abdallah.

"What about when I am *five-months* pregnant?" Hasna laughed.

"*Only,* if I am *also* under the tree with Abdallah catching figs!" They were two children playing at being husband and wife, and Abdallah was their child.

In spite of the morning glasses of olive oil, and the nightly mounting of Sabha, *she had not swallowed a fly.* Each month when she got her period, she despaired. With her mother as chaperon, she had finally gone to the shrine of Hmediye, a Moslem saint, who was believed to answer the petitions of women. Sabha prayed at the shrine that her barrenness would be over.

Her mother secretly feared that Awad would divorce her, or take a second, *fertile,* wife! She told her daughter that she believed that someone had given Sabha the *evil eye.*

Blue eyes were thought to be especially *evil*; the only person she knew with blue eyes was *Hasna! "Hasna must be responsible for my barrenness,"* she thought. *"She envies me because I am beautiful."*

The day after Sabha's return from the shrine, Hasan happened to be visiting. Sabha looked at Hasna, round with the child she was carrying. She looked at the smile on Hasna's freckled face. She looked at her *evil blue eyes.* Picking up the pot of coffee she had just brewed, she threw the scalding coffee into Hasna's face! Most of it landed on her *thob.*

Hasna was startled and immediately raised her hands to her smarting face. She was in so much pain that she didn't utter a word.

"You are evil," she screamed. "I am childless because of *you!*"

Salma hurriedly got a basin of water and a rag for Hasna; then she slapped Sabha across the face.

"Your barrenness has *nothing* to do with Hasna! You have been listening to Old Wives' tales. Conception is a gift from God."

Tiny blisters had started to form on Hasna's chin. Salma cleaned the tender flesh with the wet rag. She went and got a jar of honey that her father, who kept bees, had sent, and gently put a drop of honey on each red spot. Luckily, the scalding coffee had not splashed into her eyes.

"You will be fine, *binti;* these will heal and not even leave a mark."

Hasna tried to laugh, though the burns were painful. "No one will see the marks anyway because of all the freckles!"

Hasna drew her head shawl over the lower part of her face. "I must be getting back, *Yum'ma.*"

As she passed Sabha she stopped. "I daily pray that you will be blessed with a child. You have *nothing* to fear from me."

Im Mansur was worried when she saw Hasna's face. "What happened, *binti!*" she exclaimed.

"There was an accident with the coffee. I am fine, *Mart Ammie,* really I am. *Im'me* cleaned my face and put healing honey on the blisters."

That night in bed, she told Mansur about the *'accident.'* "Sabha thinks I have given her the *evil eye.* She thinks that she cannot conceive because I have *looked* at her with my blue eyes." Hasna's tears gently ran over the reddened, blistered flesh.

Mansur held her. "You *know* that that is all nonsense? There is *nothing* evil about your blue eyes. I suspect that the angels themselves have *blue eyes!*"

Hasna smiled through her tears. "You mean you don't secretly wish that you had a black-eyed wife, with raven tresses, and skin burnished like copper?"

"I wouldn't exchange my red haired beauty with her blue eyes and freckles for a *hundred* dusky, Bedouin beauties."

Hasna laughed and squeezed him. "Would you exchange me for *four?* That's all you are entitled to at one time."

"Hmm, *four?* Now that *is* something to give one pause. Hasna? Four?" Mansur seemed to be weighing the two options.

"I'd much rather have Hasna!" he said as he gently cradled her sore face against his chest.

Hasna was three months into her fourteenth year when she went into labor. It was February, cold and rainy. She had gotten so big that she used to ask Abdallah, "Do you see my feet, *habeebee?*"

He would bend over and look, leaning his curly head against her belly, to *see* if she really did still have feet.

Abdallah had lived with them nine months; Awad never even asked any more when he was coming home.

Hasna had been present in the birthing room only once – and even then not for long. She didn't quite know what to expect –except for *pain!* When the first contractions started, she would pause and wait until they had passed, and then she would continue with her work. She knew that the labor could go on for hours, and that she should keep moving for as long as she could. She tried to be calm, but she was terrified.

Im Mansur had sent for Salma, the midwife, and two of the neighbor women who had passed menopause. As the day wore on, she sent her husband and Mansur to the coffeehouse; her younger children to her sister's, and Abdallah to Helweh. (It hadn't even crossed her mind to send Abdallah to Sabha.)

The neighbor women had carried in the birthing stone upon which Hasna would sit. They had brought in a *quffeh* full of dirt to spread on the floor; Im Mansur had at hand a bundle of clean rags, a bottle of olive oil, and an earthenware dish of salt.

Hasna paced and paced and clutched her mother's and mother-in-law's hands when a contraction rent her body. There were times when she was certain that she was dying; there were times that she *wished she had died* and the pain was over.

Six hours into her labor, she was hit with an irresistible desire to *push.*

"I think the baby is ready to come," she gasped. *"It's either that, or I really am dying!"* she thought.

Im Hussein lifted Hasna's skirt and saw the black-haired head.

Hasna raised herself off the birthing stone and braced her back against the backs of the two hefty neighbor women. The neighbor women had put their arms around each other's shoulders to from a solid wall against which Hasna could push. Im Mansur raised Hasna's arms high above her head. Salma held her belly on either side.

"Push, *binti,* push," Im Hussein said. "Now rest; breathe deeply. Now push again!"

Hasna strained, her red, freckled cheeks looked like balloons as she huffed and puffed.

"Now rest; that's it; breathe deeply; that's it; now *push!*" Im Hussein instructed.

Hasna gave one more mighty push and Im Hussein caught the wet, red, silent infant before his head could hit the stone.

There was no need to smack him on the buttocks, he had come into the world silently, but fully awake – blinking the trauma of his journey from dark eyes.

She laid the placid baby on Hasna's belly. His little fists waved in the air. His eyes were opened wide. His legs quivered in the cold.

Hasna cradled him against her breast. She ran soothing hands over his arms, his legs, his head. His black hair was long enough to part and wetly clung to his head in damp ringlets.

Im Hussein cut the cord and tied off the stump. She took the baby from Hasna's chest and passed him to Im Mansur to clean, to oil, and to rub with salt.

With Salma pressing on her belly, and Hasna pushing, the afterbirth was expelled. The neighbor women swept up the bloody dirt from the floor and took it, along with the afterbirth wrapped in a rag, outside to bury.

Im Mansur passed the oiled and salt-rubbed infant to Salma to swaddle. Salma placed the baby on the white swaddling rags she had covering her knees. She pulled down his sturdy arms next to his body; she straightened his sturdy legs and securely wrapped him so he looked like a butterfly still in its cocoon. She wound the long strip of cloth around the swaddled infant and tied it so he couldn't kick off the swaddling.

He looked at his Sitteh- his grandmother, with dark, questioning eyes. The neighbor women had washed Hasna and dressed her in a clean shift. They had helped her move to a pallet so that she could rest her back against the wall.

Salma passed Hasna the infant wrapped in his cloth cocoon. Hasna opened her shift and guided the searching mouth to her nipple. His little head jerked as he frantically sought for the tit. Hasna placed a nipple in his mouth. It was painful as he took hold and began to suck.

"That's it, *habeebee*," she said. "That's it," she cooed as she ran a loving hand over the back of his little head. "That's it *Omar;* that's it, *Yum'ma.*"

She had given birth to her first son. He was named after his paternal grandfather. From this day forth he would be known as *Omar ibn Mansur ibn Omar.*

Im Hussein went to the coffeehouse to announce the baby's arrival. She called out to Mansur, using his new title, *Abu Omar.*

"Ya, Abu Omar," she called smiling broadly. "The *bridegroom* has come!"

The boy that he was, Mansur went up to the aged midwife and kissed her on both cheeks and put half a dinar in her palm. The men in the coffeehouse smiled and applauded. Im Hussein had delivered Mansur, and now Mansur's son! It was a proud day when a man, even though he was only eighteen, became the father of a son.

Chapter 12

Sabha could not contain her jealousy; it spilled over into everything she did, everything she thought; she was possessed as though possessed by a *jinn. How dare,* red haired, blue-eyed, freckled-faced Hasna have given birth to a *beautiful baby boy,* while *she,* raven haired, black-eyed, blemish-free Sabha was barren! It wasn't fair!

She wanted to *hurt* Hasna. She wanted to *punish* Hasna. *What better way to hurt and punish Hasna than to take Abdallah from her.* "I will speak to Awad tonight," she said out loud to herself. "I will tell him that it is time that Abdallah came *home,* that *I* will take care of him. I will get at Hasna through Abdallah." Sabha smiled to herself to think how she would *hurt* Abdallah and thereby *punish* Hasna.

That night she *did* broach the subject with Awad. "Now that Hasna has her own son, *habeebee,* don't you think it time that Abdallah come home to us?"

"*You* want to take care of Abdallah?" Awad asked.

"Of course, he is your son, and I am his father's wife. *I should be the one* taking care of him, not your sister." Sabha asserted. "Am *I* not as good a mother as Hasna?" she pouted. "Perhaps if I had Abdallah to care for, my womb would open and I would be able to conceive."

"Let me think about it," Awad said.

"There is *nothing* to think about! Tomorrow you must go and bring Abdallah here!"

When Awad tried to lift the skirt of her nightgown, she put a restraining hand on his. "*First* Abdallah!" she cooed as she rolled over on her side.

The next morning Awad went to see Hasna and Mansur.

Hasna was sitting on the daybed in the sitting room. She was nursing Omar and Abdallah was cuddled next to her. She had one arm around Abdallah and in the other she cradled Omar. Awad paused at the door, momentarily touched by the picture Hasna and the children made.

When she saw Awad at the door, she covered her breast and the nursing Omar with her shawl. She smiled at her brother and beckoned him in.

"Your timing is perfect, *Mart Ammie* is just making tea and Mansur has gone to get some seed cakes. He'll be right back."

"How is the little one doing?" Awad asked.

"He is hungry all the time. What an appetite he has, *ma'shallah.*"

"Now that you have your own son, it is time for me to take Abdallah back. He has stayed with you long enough."

"Take him back? But he is still so little, and he is *no trouble at all.* He is only three; next year when he is four he will be able to go with Saif and Ali when they tend the goats and sheep. *Please* Awad let him stay with us until he is four." There were tears in her eyes, and panic in her heart, as she pleaded with her brother.

"No, you have enough on your hands. *It is not right* that my son be raised in the house of my sister. Sabha will be his mother now. When you have finished nursing Omar, you can go and gather his things together. I will be taking Abdallah with me."

Hasna laid the sleeping Omar down in the metal cradle. Taking Abdallah by the hand she went with a heavy heart to gather his clothes together.

"Where am I going, *Yum'ma?*" Abdallah asked. He had only recently started to call her *Yum'ma* – 'mother'. It broke Hasna's heart to realize she was sending *her son* to a woman who didn't like him.

"Your father and your father's wife miss you so much that they want you to go and stay with them," Hasna said in a choked voice. "You will still come and visit me every day."

"My father's wife doesn't like me. She used to pinch me and box my ears," Abdallah said with tears in his eyes.

"That was when you were very small. Now that you are a big boy of three she is going to love you. And just think;

you will also be with Saif and Ali and Sitteh Salma. They will take care of you and love you."

"I want to stay with you, *Yum'ma,*" he cried throwing his arms around her neck.

Hasna hugged him hard. She placed his hand against her heart. "Abdallah, you are always *here* right in my heart! You are as much *my son, habeebee,* as Omar is, *Yum'ma.*"

Awad was sitting and having tea with Mansur when Hasna came back into the room with Abdallah. She put his bundle of clothes just inside the door. She sat on the daybed beside Mansur and took Abdallah into her lap. She wrapped her arms around him and held him close to her heart.

"*Please,* Awad, *please* don't take him," she begged as the tears rolled down her cheeks and into Abdallah's curls.

"We would like to keep him," Mansur said, holding one of Abdallah's hands.

"No, you have been kind enough to have cared for him all these months. It is time that he came home."

Awad wrenched his sobbing son from Hasna's arms and left. "*Yaba,* I want to stay with *Yum'ma Hasna* and *Ammie Mansur,*" he sobbed. Awad closed his ears and his heart to his son's pleas. He did not turn around to see his sister crying on Mansur's shoulder. He hardened his heart to the sounds of her weeping.

Sabha was grimly glad to see Awad return with Abdallah. She took the squirming child from him and dragged him up the stone steps. In the privacy of the upper room, she slapped him hard across the face.

"Stop that sniffling. You will listen to *me!* If you tell your father, or *Sitto,* or Saif or Ali that I slapped you, I will *beat* you with a stick. Do you understand?"

Abdallah's eyes were big and round. He was frightened. He nodded his head as he held back his sobs. He went to the far end of the room and sat in the corner. Quietly he slipped his thumb into his mouth; his tears dripped off his chin. He wanted Hasna – she was the only mother he knew.

In the two weeks that Abdallah had been back, he had not smiled once. He moved as though in a fog. He sat quietly beside Saif and Ali and never spoke. Whenever Sabha was near him, he visibly shuddered. Sometimes Sabha would force him to sit in her lap. He would sit rigidly. He never leaned back against her; he kept his hands tightly clasped in his lap, so tightly that the knuckles were white.

Sabha would pat his curls, and smiling say to Salma and Awad, "See how much Abdallah loves his new mother. He *always* wants to sit in my lap, *habeebee.*" When no one was looking she would pull the fine hairs at the back of his neck and smiling, whisper into his ear, *"You cry and I will beat you."* He would rapidly blink his eyes to get rid of the tears before anyone would notice.

Sabha had tried to arrange it so that he should *not* see Hasna, and that Hasna should *not see him*. Whenever Hasna came, Sabha would take Abdallah into the upper room and order him not to come out. She would tell Hasna that he was napping, that perhaps she could see him another day.

Salma would order her to bring Abdallah down. "He is sleeping, *Mart Ammie;* I don't want to disturb him."

"You *go* and bring him down *right now!*" Salma would order.

Sabha *did* go reluctantly to get Abdallah. She practically wrenched his arm from its socket. "When you go downstairs, you sit in *my lap.* You are not to go over to your aunt! Do you hear me!" she hissed.

When Abdallah came down the stairs, his hand grasped firmly by Sabha, he crawled into her lap and barely glanced at Hasna. When Hasna put out her arms to him, he shook his head no and hid his face against the woman he feared.

It broke Hasna's heart. She coaxed; he ignored. Finally he whispered something into Sabha's ear. She smiled and set him down. "He wants to go up and take his nap. He *so loves* being with me. He has never *once* mentioned you, Hasna. I *am his mother now!*" she gloated.

Hasna watched as Abdallah dejectedly mounted the stone steps. He looked so little, so alone. She wiped quick tears from her eyes. She couldn't see Abdallah's tears; she couldn't hear his cry of *"Yum'ma, Yum'ma."*

Abdallah became more and more withdrawn. He had to be reminded to eat. At night he had nightmares. He was losing weight and becoming listless. The energetic, happy three-year old he had been was gone.

Salma finally talked to Awad. "He is pining for Hasna. I don't know what Sabha is doing, but it is clear that he is frightened of her. She won't allow him to speak to Hasna or Hasna to hold him. She pretends that Abdallah *doesn't* want anything to do with Hasna.

"What do you mean Hasna can't hold him or speak to him? Doesn't she come every day?"

"Hasna does come every day. And every day Sabha forces him to sit in her lap and not talk to her. She told Hasna that he never even asks about her."

"I will see about that!" Awad said angrily.

Sabha had not expected Awad to be home. She had just finished beating Abdallah when Awad opened the door. The belt was still in her hand; the sweat was still on her brow; his son was huddled in a corner too frightened to cry.

"Awad...I...." Sabha stammered.

"Not *one word! Not one!* I will deal with you later."

Awad picked up Abdallah and left the room.

"*Yum'ma,* go and gather up Abdallah's clothes and bring them to Hasna's."

Abdallah clung to his father's neck and quietly cried. There were tears in Awad's eyes as he walked the short distance to Hasna's house in the village.

He rapped on the courtyard door. When Mansur opened it, he was surprised to see Awad standing there with Abdallah in his arms.

"Come in, come in," Mansur said standing aside so Awad could enter.

"Where is Hasna?" Awad asked.

"Awad? I am here," Hasna said as she came into the courtyard.

"I have brought Abdallah," was all that Awad could say.

When Abdallah heard Hasna's voice, he lifted his head from his father's shoulder. He looked at Hasna and put his arms out to her, *"Yum'ma...Yum'ma!"* he sobbed.

Hasna took him in her arms. He wrapped his arms around her neck and his legs around her waist. His body was racked with a shuddering sigh as he nestled his head against her neck.

Hasna and Mansur looked questioningly at Awad.

"Abdallah belongs here with you," he said. "I am intrusting my son to you. I will come to see him every day, but he is never to see Sabha."

Awad went up and kissed his son's hand. "I will never take you away again, *ibnee*. You belong with *Amto* Hasna and *Ammo* Mansur. Abdallah turned his face and smiled at his father as he reached out and patted the stubble on his chin.

It was a sober, angry Awad who confronted Sabha. "Pack your things; I am returning you to your father's house. *I divorce you. I divorce you. I divorce you.*"

The formula was simple. All he had to do was tell her three times that he divorced her, and they were divorced.

Sabha smiled as she gathered her things together. "I will send my brothers for my bridal chest. I am frankly glad to be done with you. Perhaps now I can marry a *real* man, a man who will give me children."

It was then that he picked up the belt with which she had beaten Abdallah and beat her.

Chapter 13

The seasons came and went. There were plantings and harvests. The child-bride, Hasna, was no longer a child. She was eighteen and the mother of three sons: Omar, Khalil, and Kareem. Four, if one considered Abdallah who still made his home with Hasna and Mansur. Mansur was now twenty-three.

There had been other changes in the five years since Hasna and Mansur were wed. Awad had married for the third time. This time the girl, Laila, was a young widow who had a son. Her son stayed with her late husband's family, but they didn't want Laila; they insisted that she return to her father's home. She was reluctantly persuaded to marry Awad; her own family didn't want an unmarried daughter at home either.

Awad wanted a wife who *looked nothing* like Miryam or Sabha. He also wanted a wife who was a proven *breeder.* Laila was fair, petite, and quiet. She did whatever Salma or Awad asked her without complaint or comment. Unfortunately, there were no children, and Awad had to admit, at least to himself, that *he* was to blame; though he *did* continue to drink a glass of olive oil each morning.

Sabha had married an older man who was a widower with young children. In the four years she had been married, she had given birth to three girls. Hasna had once passed her in the market. She was shocked in the change in Sabha. Sabha looked old and worn-out. She had put on considerable weight and was missing several teeth. They passed without speaking.

The most wonderful change was in Abdallah. He was now a boisterous six. He was old enough to accompany his young uncles, Saif and Ali, when they took the herd of sheep and goats to graze. He was solicitous and kind to his little *brothers,* Omar and Khalil, and even condescended to hold the baby, Kareem, when his *mother,* Hasna, was especially busy. He saw his father, Awad, almost every day, but he had taken to also calling Mansur, *Yaba.* He was a happy child; quick to obey; quick to give hugs. His love for Hasna knew no bounds.

Hasna had always been a hard worker. She was inquisitive and hungered to learn new things. Her mother Salma was skilled in making *khawabi* –the mud-bins used for storage; Im Mansur was an accomplished potter. From these two women, Hasna learned to make pottery.

In the towns, men were the potters and used a potter's wheel; in the villages the craft of making pots was a female occupation and no wheel was used.

Hasna learned from her mother and mother-in-law how to dig the clay rock out of the ground; she learned how to grind it using heavy stone rollers; she learned how to sift it, weigh it, and add the correct portions of straw, sand, and powdered pottery shards.

The mixture was then kneaded like bread dough with just enough water added to make the *dough* workable. She learned by watching and doing. Both Salma and Im Mansur were good teachers.

The piece to be made was put on a straw mat. A flat bottom was made and smoothed. Gradually sides were added and smoothed with a shard of old pottery. It was then left to dry in the sun. Once it was dry, another layer was added and the pot was built up; again it was left to dry. Sometimes handles were added. Sometimes designs were painted on the sides. Large vessels were made to hold water and olive oil; small cooking pots were made; there were water jugs and even the shallow basin used for ritual ablutions before prayer.

Once all the pots were shaped, they were left to dry in the summer sun for two or three weeks. At the end of that period they were put in a fire pit filled with brush and cow dung cakes. The fire was kept going for about two hours. Once the fire had cooled, the pots were removed – hopefully only a few had broken.

Hasna would take her four sons and two little brothers and go on *brush-gathering* excursions. She had made a crude sling out of a scrap of burlap so she could carry the baby, Kareem, across her chest. Two-year-old Khalil would ride on the shoulders of Ali, and four-year-old Omar on the shoulders of Saif. Six-year-old Abdallah had the honor of leading the donkey and carrying the basket with their lunch in it.

Hasna would set Kareem down on a burlap sack and Saif, Ali, and Abdallah would *fence* him in with a crude stone corral. It wasn't very high, but just high enough that he couldn't crawl out. Hasna would give him a hard piece of dry bread to chew, and then she and the boys made a game of gathering brush, always keeping Kareem in sight.

Once they had gathered all the brush that the donkey could carry, Hasna broke out the lunch.

The children sat around Kareem and ate sandwiches stuffed with white cheese and cucumber; sandwiches spread with homemade apricot jam; they drank homemade yogurt and ate kumquats that Hasna had picked fresh from the tree in the courtyard– and still seemed to taste of summer sun.

On the way back to the village, Omar and Khalil would perch on the pile of brush. Hasna would spread the burlap sack on the top so the brush would not prick the boys' tender legs. Saif and Ali walked on either side of the donkey, a protective hand on the leg of a little nephew. Abdallah would lead the donkey and hold hands with Hasna.

Sometimes walking back they would sing; sometimes Hasna would tell them wonderful stories that she had heard.

Once there was an old woman who lived with her cat. The old woman brought home a bowl of milk, which the cat quickly lapped up.

The old woman was so mad that she cut off the tail of the cat.

The cat said, 'Meow, meow, please sew my tail back on." Hasna was good at making all the sounds and changing the voices.

The old woman said, 'Give me back my milk and I will sew your tail back on."

"How was the cat going to give the Old Woman back her milk?" Saif asked. "And sew its tail back on?"

Well, the old woman pointed to a ewe in the field and told the cat to go and get milk from the ewe.

"How can a cat talk to a ewe?" Ali questioned. "A cat *can't talk!* And a cat can't milk a ewe!"

"This was a special cat who could talk to all kinds of animals; and his paws were perfect for milking. He could even talk to people," Hasna said.

So he asked the ewe. The ewe said 'yes', but first she wanted a branch from a tree.

The cat went to the tree and asked for a branch. The tree said 'yes,' but first the cat must ask the farmer plowing the field to plow under the tree.

"*Yum'ma,* trees can't talk!" Omar laughed.

The cat asked the plowman. He also said 'yes,' but first he wanted a pair of new shoes.

The cat went to the cobbler and asked for a pair of shoes for the plowman, who would plow under the tree, which would give him a branch for the ewe, who would give him milk for the old woman who would then sew his tail back on.

The cobber said 'yes,' but first he wanted two loaves of bread from the baker woman.

The cat went to the baker woman and asked for two loaves of bread to give to the cobbler, who would give him the shoes to give to the plowman, who would plow under the tree, which would give him a branch to give to the ewe, who would then give him milk to give to the Old Woman who would sew his tail back on.

The baker woman said 'yes,' but first she wanted a bucket of manure.

The cat gave her the bucket of manure and then...

Saif and Ali and Abdallah, laughing, joined in chorus saying:

The baker woman gave him the loaves, which he gave to the cobbler, who gave him the shoes which he gave to the plowman, who plowed under the tree, which gave the branch to the cat, who gave it to the ewe, who gave him the milk which he gave to the Old Woman, who sewed his tail back on!

"*Ma'shallah,* how clever you *all* are to have remembered everything *exactly* in order," Hasna laughed. "You *must* have heard the story before!"

Mansur was standing in the open door of the courtyard when Hasna and the boys returned home. He took the sleeping Kareem from his burlap sling and nestled him on his shoulder. Two-year old Khalil tugged on his *umbaz* and wanted to be held as well. Abdallah, holding Omar's hand and leading the donkey with the other, guided the donkey to the side of the house where he and Saif and Ali unloaded the brush they had collected. It had been a *wonderful outing.*

"You look like you had a good afternoon," Mansur said smiling at Hasna.

"We had a wonderful time. We had a picnic; we sang songs; we told stories, *and* of course we collected brush to use in the fire pit."

"*Yaba,* Khalil and I got to *ride* on the donkey!" Omar said excitedly as he came around the corner. "We sat like princes on a pile of brush!" he beamed.

"Princes don't sit on a brush pile, *Yaba;* they sit on fine silk cushions stuffed with wool."

"*Yum'ma* also told us a story about a cat which could talk and needed to have his tail sewn on, but first had to return a bowl of milk to an Old Woman," Abdallah said.

"If you are *really* good, *Yaba,*" Abdallah smiled, "I'll tell you the story over dinner."

The children slept well that night, as Hasna said, *bedun hez* – they didn't need to be *rocked.* Abdallah, Omar, and Khalil were almost asleep as soon as their heads hit the pillow. The three of them slept on the same pallet with Khalil in the middle (because he was the youngest of the three and tended to roll off the mattress.)

Kareem still slept in the metal cradle beside Hasna's side of the thin mattress. It was wonderful to finally be able to go to bed. Mansur had turned on his side, after kissing Hasna good-night, and was almost asleep. Hasna spooned around him. He reached behind him and pulled one of her long red braids over his chest. He kissed the end of it before falling into a sleep where he dreamt of a tailless cat which could talk to a plowman and carry a pail of manure.

Chapter 14

The end of four hundred years of Ottoman Rule, the beginning of the British Mandate, and the end of World War I had all been contributing factors to the impoverishment of the Palestinian countryside.

The Ottomans had levied high taxes on land and agricultural produce, forcing many farmers to borrow money from unscrupulous moneylenders using their land as collateral. The Ottomans had also conscripted men into the Turkish army based on the names on tax rolls. Some farmers, to avoid their own names appearing on tax records, asked urban lawyers and notables to register the land in *their names*. So, legally, on paper the farmers' land *belonged* to the lawyer or urban notable. The farmers were not aware of the legal ramifications of their acts. In some cases it literally meant that the farmer was working land that had been in his family for generations, but legally was *owned* by a distant absentee landowner. In all practicality, the farmer became a *tenant* farmer on his own land.

Peasant indebtedness grew. The moneylenders had to be paid; the urban landowners had to be paid; the farmer had to pay the grain merchant for the seed he had bought on credit; taxes had to be paid.

Agriculture at the best of times was a risky business. There was drought or intense rain; there was poor, overworked soil that resulted in meager harvests; the roads were in ill-repair and it was difficult to transport crops to market; the market was flooded with cheap Syrian and Egyptian wheat which meant the Palestinian villager got little profit from his own wheat. His primitive way of farming: *broadcasting* the seed – tossing it over the plowed soil; cutting the wheat harvest with sickles; threshing it by having mules walk over it; winnowing it with wooden pitchforks; sifting it by hand; the lack of irrigation – all contributed to poor yields.

The peasant worked hard, but realized *little* from his work – sometimes nothing. He couldn't pay his taxes; he couldn't pay the moneylenders; he couldn't pay the absentee landowner; he struggled to feed his family. Sometimes animals were confiscated in lieu of payment. That was how Mansur became a mule.

Abu Mansur had bought seed on credit. He had promised the grain merchant that once the crop was harvested and sold he would pay him what he owed. He had all hopes of doing so.

Hasna, Im Mansur, and Mansur's brother Khalil's young wife had sowed the seed by hand; *broadcasting* it much like women had done in ancient times. It was almost Biblical: *some fell on rocky soil and died, and some fell on fertile soil and took root.*

They had walked up and down the rows of plowed earth and tossed the seed; the overturned earth warm on their bare feet. Abu Mansur, Mansur, and his brother Khalil had followed in their stead and with short-handled spades pulled dirt over the sown seeds. It was back-breaking work; but it was how it had been done for hundreds of years; they farmed as they knew.

Every day they prayed for rain. Every day the sky was clear and cloudless. The rains finally did come, but were sporadic and sparse. The wheat grew, but not very tall and not much of it. The grain, once cut and threshed, winnowed and sifted, bagged and taken to market, when sold was not enough to pay all who needed paid.

The grain merchant sent three burly men to confiscate the mule in lieu of what was owed him.

Mansur and Khalil stood with fists clenched in frustration as the mule was lead away.

How would they be able to plow the fields in November if there were no mule to pull the plow? They had argued with the three men, but it was like spitting words into the wind. Other men had also lost their plow mules.

When November did roll around, the fields lay fallow. They had kept back enough seed from the previous planting, so seed was not the problem; the problem was how to turn the soil; how to break up the clods and prepare the field for planting; how *to plow*.

Hasna found Mansur in the *qa'albayt* sharpening the plowshare. He sat on a low stool, and with a file was working the blade so it would cut through the earth like a burnished knife cut through bread dough.

"Why are you sharpening the blade?" she asked as she laid a hand on his shoulder.

"The field needs to be plowed," was all he said.

She spoke the obvious. "We have no mule to pull the plow. The neighbors have no mules to pull their plows. The donkey is too small; what do you intend to do?"

"I intend to *pull the plow* myself. Khalil can push and direct; I can pull," he answered grimly.

"*You're going to pull the plow!*"

"Of course, I'm almost as strong as a mule," he tried to smile.

He looped the reins of the harness around his chest. He bent almost in half straining, muscles bulging; legs trembling. The plow only moved an inch or two with Khalil pushing. He tried again, and again, and again. Both he and Khalil were cursing under their breath.

Hasna, watching from the side of the field, handed the baby Kareem to Abdallah. "Hold him, *Yum'ma.*"

She walked across the field, the ground hot and hard beneath her bare feet. She looked at her husband and at her brother-in-law. "Why don't you *both* pull and *I'll* push?"

"You can't push the plow," Mansur stated. "It's man's work."

Hasna laughed, though she was a little perturbed. *"Man's work*, is it? I can gather the harvest, and broadcast the seed; I can pick fruit, and make baskets, and pots, and weave rugs, but *I can't plow?* If *you can be a mule*, I can learn to push a plow."

Her freckles seemed to stand out when she was angry. A slow grin spread across Mansur's and Khalil's faces.

"It *would* be easier if we both pulled," Khalil said. "We can pull the plow in the direction it should go, all Hasna has to do is push."

"All?" Hasna asked, just a little indignantly. "You need to remember, *my dears, you two are the mules; I am the plowman!"* she laughed.

Khalil and Mansur divided the harness between them. They dug their bare feet into the hard ground and *pulled*. The plow at first protested, and then started to cut through the hard soil. Hasna pushed; the warm, plowed earth squished between her toes, the dirt got under the nails.

The hot sun beat down on their bowed heads. Sweat poured off their faces and dampened the clothes they were wearing. They completed one row, and then turned and plowed the next. Up and down the field they went.

Abdallah had gone back to the house with Kareem and had given him to Im Mansur. He took a bucket of cool water from the *zir*, and along with a metal cup went back to the field. Mansur, Khalil and Hasna would stop for a moment to quench their thirst and then once again pull the sharpened plow share through the well-packed earth.

By dusk they were exhausted and could hardly move, but the field was plowed. The next day, Hasna, Im Mansur and Khalil's wife would *broadcast* the seed; Abdallah, Saif and Ali would follow them and with their spades turn the warm earth over the pregnant seed.

That night in bed, Mansur and Hasna could barely move. It seemed as though their muscles were *remembering* the strain of plowing. The muscles in their legs ached. There were burn marks on Mansur's shoulders from where the harness had rubbed against the skin. Hasna's hands were blistered from grasping the handles of the wooden plow. She found it difficult to draw her fingers close to her palm.

"*We* did it, *illhumdillah,*" Mansur smiled exhaustedly. "*We* actually did it," he signed, rightly proud.

"If the crop is good this year, perhaps we will have enough to buy a mule. It *would* be easier with a mule," he sleepily said as he began to doze off.

Hasna, her head on his shoulder, was nodding off. "Though you *do* make a handsome *mule,*" she murmured as she finally slept.

Chapter 15

The British, though organized and precise, were really not much better than the Ottomans. Their special relationship with historic Judaism had allowed them to sympathize with, and sometimes turn a blind eye to, Jewish immigration. Lord Balfour had been pivotal in signing a document, called the *Balfour Declaration* which allowed for the creation of a Jewish homeland in Palestine. The declaration was signed in 1917, the year the Turks were driven out of Palestine, the year that the British Mandate began, the year that Hasna was born.

By 1936 there had been an *adjustment* on the part of Palestinians to the Mandate. Many in the city saw British rule as *tolerable.* Those who spoke English well, were the graduates of private English-speaking institutions, saw possible *advancement* in government-related jobs. Some sought to be *British* in the way they acted; in the décor of their homes; in the way they dressed. Many people in urban areas adopted English-style dress; some of the older men still wore the red pill-box shaped *fez or tarboosh* that had been made popular by their Ottoman occupiers. Some men stopped wearing the *tarboosh* and adopted the fedora worn by sophisticated British businessmen that they saw pictured in newspapers, magazines, and in films. The *distance* between a city-dweller in his western dress, speaking his citified Arabic, reading English novels, and the often illiterate, village peasant in his/her traditional dress wearing a *kuffiyeh* on his head, speaking a rural dialect, became wider. Some urbanites *looked down* on the peasant as being socially *inferior,* while *looking up* to the British as being superior – almost someone to *envy.*

Jewish immigration continued. Some lands on the coast were actually *sold* to Zionists – sold by some farmers who couldn't pay their debts; sold by some unscrupulous moneylenders and lawyers who had no deep attachment to the land and saw it as a *tradable commodity.* It seemed there was no *sense of shame* for Arab land brokers who sold Palestinian land to Jewish immigrants.

There was a gradual *awakening* of the peasants to the realization that they were being ill-treated by the Mandate political regime; had certainly been ill-treated by the Turkish regime; and were, in many cases, being looked-down upon and ill-treated by the urban *effendi* class.

The ground was fertile for a peasant rebellion against the British Mandate government, against the subtle encroaching Zionism, even against the urban elites and some of their own village leaders. The peasants, who had been marginalized and impoverished, became willing actors in the staging of a popular rebellion. As a reaction to their being anti-British and anti-Zionist, they became more conservative disparately wanting to hold onto their peasant culture and identity as Palestinian.

A violent, peasant-initiated resistance, directed at British colonial rule and Jewish immigration and land acquisition, began in 1936, the year that Hasna and

Mansur's new two-room house was built, the year their son Jameel was born, and the year the coffeehouse got a radio!

Abu Mansur had learned a valuable lesson with the confiscation of the mule – he never bought grain on credit again. *Illhumdillah,* no one in the village had mortgaged their land; no one in the village had had their land registered in other names than their own. If cash was needed, young men from the village hired themselves out as day laborers in Jerusalem. (Though even here, they were to discover, the British Mandate government had set the minimum wage for Arab workers below that of Jewish workers.)

With two married sons, Abu Mansur felt the necessity of building two small stone houses, one for each son. The men in the village did the actual construction using stones from the surrounding mountainside. The women in the village carried the pebbles and small stones that were used as filler and the buckets of water that were used to mix the mortar. Awad, Hasna's brother, who had been an apprentice to their father, Abdallah, supervised the erection of his sister's home.

Each of the two rooms had an outside door and two long, barred windows. It was on one level. There was no *qa'albayt* for animals, no upper level where the family lived and slept. Each of the rooms had a dome roof. The family continued to live in one room; thin mattresses were stored in a curtained alcove during the day and spread on the floor at night. The second room was used as a sitting room for guests, and would eventually become the living quarters for their oldest son, Omar, when he married.

The stone window ledges were broad enough for Hasna to set a primus on when she cooked; wide enough to set the wooden bread bowl – the *batiyeh*--on when she put the dough in the sun to rise; spacious enough for her to sit and watch the sunrise over the hills as she nursed a hungry infant.

She loved the fact that there were *two* tall windows in each room. Once the wooden shutters were opened, the room was flooded with sun. The home of her childhood and the house of the first years of her marriage were dark – these sun-drenched rooms were a little *glimpse into heaven* she thought.

She left the windows unshuttered until they had finished their evening meal. It was soothing to her spirit to sit around the large straw tray on the floor upon which their evening meal was spread; it was soothing to her spirit to see the faces of Mansur and those of her five sons, *five* because she always counted her nephew, Abdallah, as one of her own children; it was soothing to her spirit to see the last rays of the setting sun soften the interior of the house and hide any unimaginable blemish – for to Hasna, the house was perfect.

When the houses were being built, one for Mansur, the second for Khalil, both Mansur and Khalil had hired out as day laborers in the city. Hard money was needed, and this was the easiest way for the men to obtain it. It was this working with other villagers --day laborers like themselves -- that they learned of the oppressive measures in other villages; that they learned of the differences in minimum wages paid to Arab and Jewish workers; that they learned of the growing unrest and began to feel the first undercurrents of resistance.

But, it was the appearance of a *radio* in the coffeehouse that wrought the biggest change in the peasant's attitude toward the Mandate, Jewish immigration, and their own plight.

Every evening after work the men would gather in the coffeehouse to play *sheish-beish* (backgammon), drink pungent Turkish coffee, and *listen* to the radio. Most men in the village, with the exception of the *Imam* and *mukhtar* were illiterate; they couldn't read, but there was nothing wrong with their *hearing.* They heard news from Egypt where there were negotiations between the United Kingdom and Egypt; they heard news from Syria of a general strike against the French occupation; they heard news from Jerusalem of the confiscation of a cache of arms destined for Zionist militants.

It was on the radio that they learned of the April 15, 1936 attack on a convoy of trucks in which two Jewish drivers were shot and killed by Arab assailants. It was on the radio that they learned of the revenge attack by Jewish gunmen who killed two Arab workers. It was on the radio that they learned of Jewish rioters beating Arab children in response to the killing of the two Jewish truck drivers. It was on the radio that they learned that a General Strike of all Arab workers had been called.

The radio brought the news of the formation of the Arab Higher Committee which appealed to all Arabs to continue the strike until the Mandate Government met its demands: the prohibition of Jewish immigration; the prohibition of Arab lands being sold to Jews; the formation of a National Government responsible to a representative council. The leadership went on to say that there should be no payment of taxes until Jewish immigration was stopped. The seeds of rebellion had been sown.

The radio reported the visit of Lord Peel to Mandatory Palestine, and of his recommendation that Palestine be partitioned into a small Jewish state and a larger Arab state linked to Trans-Jordan. It was the first time that *transfer* of Palestinian Arabs from a new Jewish state to an Arab state linked to Trans-Jordan was officially mentioned. The news caused the formation of militant bands of partisans and of armed insurrection that targeted British holdings and Jewish settlements.

In spite of the political turmoil which engulfed the country, there were breathtaking sunrises and sunsets; Kareem had begun to talk, and Jameel had begun to crawl; there was bread to be made and clothes to be washed; there was water to fetch from the well and brush to be gathered; there were five little boys to nurture and a husband to care for. Hasna's world was wrapped in a cocoon of domesticity. She didn't have time for politics; Mansur did!

Mansur, as most of the men in the village, spent every evening at the coffeehouse listening to the radio and discussing the *"situation"*. One evening when Mansur and Khalil arrived at the coffeehouse there was a stranger sitting alone drinking tea. His head was wrapped in a white *kuffiyeh* and he wore a heavy beard and moustache that hid his cheeks and mouth. He had piercing black eyes and a hawk nose.

He listened with the others to the news on the radio. Wiping his lips with a finger and brushing his drooping moustache he spoke:

"What do we intend to do about this, my brothers? Every day our British occupiers put new restrictions; every day there are new Jewish immigrants invading our country, buying our land, setting up settlements."

"What can we do?" Mansur ventured.

"We can resist. We can rebel. We can fight the occupier and the Zionist invasion." The stranger's voice rose; he became quite animated as he struck his right fist into his left palm.

"You can be *trained* to be fighters. What one of you does not have a hunting rifle at home? What house does not have a scythe for cutting wheat? What farmer among you does not have a saw or hoe or rake?" The stranger looked around at the faces of the men watching him – listening to what he had to say.

"All of these things can be used as weapons," he paused.

"I am here to recruit fighters, to train men how to make bombs; to train men how to fight the British and the immigrants."

"Who are you? Where do you come from?" Khalil asked.

"For the moment, it is better that you do not know my name or from what village I come. It is only important that you know that *I am like you.*" Once again a rough finger moved across his lips beneath the canopy of bristling moustache.

"Think about what I have said. I will be back to see who among you would be interested in joining our band."

"What is your band called?" Mansur asked.

The stranger smiled, "We are called *the Black Hand.*"

He finished the last of his tea and carefully set the glass down on the metal stand.

"*Salam aleikum* my brothers," he said as he disappeared into the night.

Mansur couldn't sleep that night. He felt the stirring of rebellion in the pit of his stomach. The words of the stranger had set fire to the kindling within him. He *wanted* to resist. He *wanted* to fight. He *wanted* to join the rebel band – *The Black Hand.*

Chapter 16

Hasna hauled the large, shallow, brass wash tub into the yard. She heated water on the primus and bathed, each in turn, four little boys. By the time she placed the baby, Jameel, in the *leggin* the water was tepid. He sat contentedly and splashed his hands in the water, giggling when the spray hit his face, and the water dripped off his long lashes like happy tears.

Jameel would look up at his mother and smile – showing his eight new teeth. She rubbed the hard cake of olive oil soap against the rag and slid the soapy rag over his sturdy limbs, over his head, wetting the raven curls. He would lower his face into the water and blow bubbles. With a tin cup she poured water over him, rinsing off the soap. He got out of the water reluctantly, was rubbed dry with a coarse rag and was dressed in threadbare hand-me-downs.

"Come and take your little brother," Hasna called to Abdallah.

Hasna poured the water from the *leggin* into a bucket for six-year old Omar to use later to quench the thirst of the flowering plants that grew in old rusty tins. Nothing was wasted. She set the brass wash tub against the stone wall to dry. She was barely conscious of the warmth of the sun on her bare toes.

It was the first time in all her married life that she was directly opposed to what Mansur wanted. The thought that he *might* become involved with the guerrillas was like having a thorn festering in her toe – every time she even thought about it she felt a pain around her heart. She imagined the worst: *Mansur arrested; Mansur killed; she by herself with five little boys and another baby on the way; she having to give up her children to her husband's family and returning to her brother's house; a widow at twenty bereft of husband and children.* This was *not* going to happen!

Hasna knew little of politics. The perimeters of her life were limited by house, fields and occasional excursions into the mountains to hunt for herbs and brush. In all her twenty years, she had *never* been to the city; she had *never* seen a British soldier; she had only seen a Jewish settler from a distance. All she knew about British colonialism and Jewish encroachment were the snatches of conversation she sometimes caught when Mansur and Khalil, or her brother, Awad, were talking. That had been until a few days ago when Mansur had shared the words that the stranger in the coffeehouse had spoken.

Mansur had enthusiastically talked about the man in the coffeehouse's warnings. He had spoken of *occupier* and *Zionist invader*. Mansur had spoken of how the stranger was there to *recruit* and *train fighters!*

Hasna had listened as Mansur had spoken. It wasn't so much that he was actually *speaking to her;* it was more like he was *speaking to himself.* Her head had been resting against his chest – right above his heart. She thought she could *feel* the rapid heartbeats as he spoke of the stranger; spoke about *resistance;* spoke about *rebellion.* She had ventured to whisper: *What could you do?* He had been startled by her question. *Why, I would become a fighter. I would learn how to defend my home and land from the occupier and the invader! After all, I am a man!*

Hasna had lain awake long after Mansur had fallen asleep. She could barely make out his features in the darkness, though her heart knew them by touch. She gently ran her fingertips over his broad nose, his bristly jaw, over the heavy lashes that fanned out against his cheeks. She gently pushed back one of the errant curls from his bronzed forehead. She loved him with a passion that bordered on idolatry. He was a husband, a lover, a father, a friend. He was a peasant *farmer,* not a guerrilla *fighter.*

She held him tightly as he slept. He murmured something in his sleep and rolled away from her. Hasna eased against his back and once again placed her arm around him, hugging his solid form against her, wishing to *protect* him – that was the word – against the dreams that were most likely playing in his mind.

The rooster was already heralding the morn when it seemed to Hasna that her eyes finally closed. (Though she had obviously slept somewhat before that as she had missed the morning call to prayer from the mosque.) Mansur was already up; the boys were moving on their pallets, and Jameel was wide-eyed in his metal cradle murmuring gibberish to his fingers, waiting to be nursed.

Hasna and the older boys stacked the pallets in the niche in the wall. Abdallah pumped the primus and put the water on to boil for coffee while Hasna nursed Jameel. Omar, with four-year old Khalil in tow, had placed the large straw mat on the floor and placed on it bowls of *zeit* and *zatar (olive oil and ground thyme mix)*, dishes of olives and *lebaneh (yoghurt spread)*; the loaves of bread his mother had baked the day before. All was ready for breakfast when Mansur entered the room.

Mansur was going to Jerusalem with his brother Khalil and brother-in-law Awad. The trip had been planned after the men had heard the words of the stranger. Jerusalem was only about five kilometers from the village – a nice morning's walk. They wanted to obtain first-hand news about the strike, perhaps pick up a bit of gossip about the British, the new immigrants, about events that were happening in the coastal cities. There was the *excitement* of doing something out of the ordinary. It was an *adventure* that spoke to the boy within the man. They wanted to gather stories that they could relate at the coffeehouse.

Hasna had been restless all morning. Oh, she had done her chores. Her hands seemed to *know* what to do automatically. *They* kneaded bread; drew water from the well; picked through lentils; carried pallets out to the sun; washed clothes; laid them over the wire clothesline to dry; changed soiled swaddling cloths; reached down and picked up a child and slung him on her hip. None of these things took any actual *thought*. In the back of her mind, like a thistle festering in her big toe, was the thought that *Mansur wanted to become a guerrilla fighter! He wanted to join a band of peasants called The Black Hand!*

I need a walk through the hills, she told herself. *I need to clear my mind.*

"We're going to the hills to gather brush," she told the boys.

"Abdallah, go and get the donkey. Omar, take the hands of Khalil and Kareem. While your father and uncles are off having their adventure, we are going to have an adventure too."

Abdallah picked up four-year-old Khalil, and Omar picked up two-year-old Kareem and placed them on the back of the donkey. The little boys grinned as their sturdy little legs gripped the sides of the donkey. Kareem wrapped his arms around Khalil's waist. Hasna slung the baby Jameel into a burlap sling so his curly head rested against her breast.

The boys loved these outings with Hasna. She sang; she joked; she told them stories. They loved this break in the routine. Going to the hills, gathering brush, somewhat spoke to the *man that lay hidden within the boy.*

The sun was high in the sky, yet there was a cooling breeze that swayed the stunted shrubs and gently ruffled Hasna's head shawl. The higher they climbed among the stone terraces, the lighter Hasna's spirit seemed to be. The heaviness that had plagued her night and morning was being lifted.

There were wild violets growing in the crevices at the base of the stone walls; there were wild cyclamens – *Grandfather's pipe* – growing in clusters; there were delicate flowers blooming among sharp thorns; over the thorn bush pale yellow butterflies danced. It was beautiful.

Hasna thought: *Subhan Allah, Praise God, why should I be afraid? Everything will be as Allah wishes it.*

She and the children went about gathering brush to burn for kindling. She sang as she worked. It was a song that the children knew – *ha sea'san, shu hell'ween* - about happy little chicks. Even Kareem, who was just beginning to talk, would mimic some of the words.

They had just balanced the load of kindling on the donkey's back when she heard the crying and the shouts.

She looked in the direction of the crying and saw, a short distance from her, a small blonde child. He must have been about three or four. He was sobbing as he looked about him, stumbling over the rocks. Hasna could see a young woman, coming from the new Jewish settlement on the hilltop, frantically climbing down toward him.

This side of the hill was especially steep. Hasna was afraid the child would stumble and roll down the hillside. Instructing Abdallah and Omar to watch over their younger brothers, she started up the hill toward the child.

It was so steep at one point, that she found herself practically crawling on her hands and knees. The young, foreign, woman was finding it difficult to descend the hill. In between them both, the child continued to sob.

Hasna kept waving to him to *sit down*. She called to him to *oq'od – sit,* even though she knew he probably couldn't understand her. The woman above him was also shouting at him in a language that Hasna did not know.

Hasna was the first to reach him. She sat down in the dirt beside him and drew him into her lap. He looked at her questioningly and continued to sob. She patted his back and spoke to him in words he could not understand: *"Ba'him'ish, habeebee, Ba'him'ish, Yum'ma."* (It's alright, my love. It's alright, Mama.)

The young, foreign woman finally reached the pair. As soon as the little one saw her he reached up his arms to her. She, too, sat in the dirt beside Hasna. It seems she was scolding the little boy as she hugged him. There were tears in her eyes.

She turned to Hasna and seemed to be thanking her. Hasna couldn't understand the words, but she could understand the meaning.

Hasna was the first to get up. She brushed off the back of her skirt, and smiling, patted the back of the little boy and kissed his shoulder. She smiled and nodded at the young mother, who in turn smiled and nodded at Hasna.

As Hasna descended the hill and rejoined her sons, she thought: *I have helped rescue a child and I have met a Jewish settler. I have met the 'enemy' – but she is a mother, just like me.*

If Hasna had had the ability to look into the future, and to see what would befall, she *still* would have rescued the child.

Chapter 17

Mansur, Khalil, and Awad stood stone-faced as the British policemen ran their hands up under the worn *umbazes* they wore and patted their cotton-trouser legs. They looked straight ahead as the policemen ran their hands briskly over their outstretched arms, down their sides, across their backs, over their buttocks. Their eyes did not meet those of the policemen as they even ran their hands over the *kuffiyehs* on their head. They were embarrassed. They were angry. They were humiliated.

"*Yallah,* Go!" the one policeman said in his accented Arabic. "*Yallah.* What are you waiting for?"

Without speaking a word, they lowered their arms, shuffled their feet in their sandals, and walked off. Most of the shops were closed; there were only a few people in the streets; a few *med'da'knee'ya* (city folk) in suits passed them, the red fezzes on their heads bright in the morning sun.

An old woman sat at the side of the square; a basket heaped with freshly cut cauliflowers in front of her. Her dress was worn and patched; the scant embroidery on the skirt was frayed and in places completely disappeared; wisps of white hair that had been dyed with *henna* peeked out from the colorful *mendeel* she wore; among the wrinkles on her chin the fine blue dots of a tattoo could be seen.

"Buy some cauliflower, *ib'nay,*" she called to the three men. "Freshly cut this morning."

Mansur, Khalil, and Awad were not interested in buying cauliflower, they were interested in why they had been singled out, stopped, and searched.

"Do you know why the *Anglesh affrenji* stopped us, *Khalti* (aunt)*?*" Mansur asked the old woman.

"They stopped you because you are *fellaheen.* As soon as they saw your *umbaz* and *kuffiyeh,* they knew that you were peasants."

"Why are they stopping peasants, *Khalti?*" Khalil asked.

"There is unrest in the villages; unrest among the *fellaheen;* they know there are peasant leaders recruiting a rebel army. They are *afraid* of us," the old woman toothlessly grinned, the tattoos on her chin alive.

"They don't stop the *med'da'knee'ya* in their British suits and Turkish fezzes," the old woman said, spitting on the cobblestones. "*May Allah destroy their faith,*" she mumbled under her breath. The three men were not sure whether she was cursing the British, or cursing the citified Arabs.

"How do you know these things, *Khalti?*" Awad questioned.

"I sit here every day; selling this or selling that. I sit and watch. Men pass me and talk. They don't *see* me. I am almost invisible to them – an old, ignorant, peasant woman – who takes notice of me!" she laughed.

"Talking in front of me is like talking to a cow or a mule – or so they think. I hear what the Arab men in their British suits and Turkish fezzes say; I hear what the peasant men who pass me whisper to one another. There *is* rebellion in the villages – rebel bands are being formed in the north, in the south, in the west – even in the villages here around Jerusalem. I see that the policemen *only* stop and search peasant men wearing *kuffiyehs*. They *never* stop men wearing fezzes." She paused. "We peasants should force all the men in the city to throw away their red fezzes, take off their British suits and wear traditional dress – an *umbaz* and *kuffiyeh* – then it would be harder for the British to tell who is peasant and who is not. But I am an old woman; what do I know?" she smiled raising a cauliflower in her out-stretched hand and asking the men again to buy.

The streets of the Old City were silent. The shops were shuttered. A few coffee shops were open where striking men sat and sipped pungent Turkish coffee. Mansur, Khalil and Awad took seats around a small, round, metal table. They ordered three cups of sweetened coffee. As they sat and sipped the thick, scalding brew they listened to the conversations around them.

They could only catch snatches of talk about: *night raids and house searches; about canings and floggings; about the confiscation of hunting rifles.* They heard one man say that he had heard that over 20,000 British troops had been sent to *'round up Arab bands'!*

"Surely that is an exaggeration," Awad said. "Twenty thousand soldiers to arrest peasants? It can't be true."

One man with a full beard and moustache was rolling a cigarette. His fingertips were stained; there were dark crescents under his nails. They heard him tell his companion about a picture he had seen in a newspaper. "The picture shows two Arabs wearing *kuffiyehs* sitting in a small cart *in front of a train.* I asked someone to read what was written under the picture. He told me that it said that it was the newest method used to check for explosives on the rails. If the cart with the Arabs in it blows up, then they *know* there is a bomb!"

A lone man was sitting at a table in the corner. He had the eyes and nose of a hawk – deep, dark, penetrating. His head was wrapped in a white *kuffiyeh;* a heavy beard and moustache hid his cheeks and mouth. Mansur glanced over at him. He was *staring* at them. His piercing eyes penetrating into Mansur. He was the stranger from the coffeehouse – the recruiter for *The Black Hand!*

The stranger pushed his chair away, the metal legs of the chair scraping against the stone tiles, and walked over to the table where they sat.

"*Salam aleikum.* May I join you?"

Mansur moved his hand in greeting, gesturing to the stranger to sit. He raised four fingers to the waiter and ordered four more cups of coffee. While they talked, unseen by them, a young, bareheaded youth watched and listened.

The loaves of bread had risen while Hasna and the boys had gathered brush. She sat inside the low stone *taboon* –placing the flat rounds of dough on the hot stones. The donkey had been unloaded, the brush stored next to the *taboon*. Abdallah was leading the donkey around the courtyard as little Khalil and Kareem rode on its back. Omar walked alongside the donkey with a protective arm around Kareem. Hasna could hear their gleeful laughter.

As Hasna snatched a hot loaf off the glowing rocks and hastily placed a new, unbaked round of dough on them, she thought about the foreign woman and her blonde-haired child.

She had seen the settlement on the hilltop from a distance. There was a fence surrounding it, and men with watchdogs patrolled the perimeter – or so she had been told. She had never actually *seen* one of the Jewish settlers – that is, not until this morning.

The woman did not *look* like the women whom Hasna knew. Her dress was different; she wore a close-fitting cap on her head; her skirt was short enough to see the lower part of her legs, and her shoes had *heels* on them. The little boy was certainly *different* – not so much because he had blonde hair – though that *did* make him stand out, but he was wearing a shirt that *buttoned* to short pants. Hasna had never seen anything like that before. What she noticed most about him was that his *eyes were blue* – just like hers!

The woman did not speak like the women she knew. Hasna had heard a few words of English, and what the woman was speaking did not sound like the words that Hasna had heard. There had been tears in the woman's eyes; she had been frightened for her child, just like Hasna would have been if one of her children had wandered off. In that one, very evident way she was a mother like Hasna.

That night when the children were settled and asleep, Hasna lay with her head on Mansur's chest. She listened as he talked about what had happened to them in the city. He told her about being stopped by police and searched. He related the stories he had heard at the coffeehouse. He spoke of the stranger who had told them unbelievable things.

"Hasna, he said such things. He said that the British round up all the men in a village and take them away. He said that they beat them with canes and flog the soles of their feet! He said they pen them in a dark room like animals in a stable and there is *one bucket* for them to use to relieve themselves! He said that they have even *hung* men in the street as a punishment and as a *warning* to others. Men are hung if a gun is found in their home!"

Hasna tightened her hold on Mansur. She kissed his chest above his heart.

"What does this stranger say we must do?" she tentatively asked.

Mansur paused and moistened his lips. He kissed the top of Hasna's head. "He says that we must *resist* – that we must *rebel.* He said that he would *train* us to become guerrilla fighters to fight the British and those foreigners who come to steal our land." He paused again, "He even said that there are some of our own countrymen whom we must fight."

Before Mansur dozed off, Hasna told him of her encounter with the settler woman and her blonde-haired child. He listened.

"You are *not* to go near the settlement again. Rescuing the child was a good and right thing to do, *habeeptee,* and may Allah bless you for it. But they are *not* like us. They are the enemy. Even a wild puppy – as cute and soft as it looks – has *fangs* and grows into a dog to be feared."

Hasna thought about what he said. She thought about the woman, and about the child with blue eyes – just like hers.

Chapter 18

Six-year-old Omar watched as his father wrapped his hunting rifle in a burlap sack. He looked questioningly as Mansur slipped *that* sack into yet another sack. He followed silently as Mansur carried the sack to the *qa'albayt* at his grandfather's house. He stood at the entrance to the stable where the sheep, goats, and donkey were kept and observed his father dig a hole in the straw beneath the ledge where the chickens nested. There he buried the sack, covering the place with loose straw.

"*Yaba,* why did you bury the rifle in the straw?" he asked.

Mansur, taking Omar's small hand in his, smiled and said, "This is a secret that only you and I know, son. You must *never* tell anyone where the rifle is hidden."

"I promise, *Yaba,*" Omar said as he raised his father's hand, kissed it and pressed it to his head. Then he thought, "*Yaba,* I won't tell Abdallah, not even *Yum'ma.* Would it be all right if I *whispered* it to Kareem though? He's too little and can't really talk?"

Mansur's lips twitched; there was a twinkle in his eye as he held the hand of a very *serious* Omar. "*Habeebee,* this will be a secret just between you, and me, *and* Kareem, *Yaba.*"

Omar smiled, somewhat relieved. With his dark brown eyes he looked directly at his father. "Secrets are always easier to keep if you can *share* them with at least one other person; *muz'boot?*"

Mansur squeezed Omar's hand and answered, "*Muz'boot.* You are pretty wise for only being six, *Yaba.*"

Mansur knew that it was almost impossible to keep a secret and thought: *Maybe whispering secrets into the ear of a baby is not such a bad idea.*

Hasna knew about the hiding of the rifle. In fact it had been her suggestion after she heard Mansur's tale about some peasant men being *hung* if they were found in possession of a rifle. She didn't know *where* the rifle was hidden, and didn't want to know. She wanted to honestly be able to say – if their house was *searched* – that *there was no rifle here.*

The Strike was in its second year when it *rained leaflets!* Hasna had never seen anything like it. She had gone to the village well with her sister-in-law, Zareefeh. She was just lifting the large earthenware vessel to the coil of cloth on Zareefeh's head, when the women heard a low-flying plane.

Startled, they both looked up just as the small plane dropped hundreds of white papers! The papers fluttered and flew and were buffeted by the breeze, finally coming to rest in the branches of trees, on the top of stone walls, looking like white *flags* in the newly planted fields and along the dirt paths of the village.

Several landed at the feet of the women at the well. Hasna and Zareefeh picked up two of the papers. One side was clear, on the other words were printed. They folded the papers very small and slipped them into their cloth sashes. Neither woman could *read*; they knew of no *woman* who could read. The *Imam* and the *mukhtar* were the only men they knew who were literate.

They wound their way up the gentle slope to the village, balancing, by moving their necks slowly side-to-side, the heavy water jugs that rested on a coil of cloth on their heads; the dust from the path coated their bare feet.

Hasna remembered her great-grandmother praying each night that when she died she wished she would be blessed with *the dust from the path still on her feet.* (Meaning she wanted to die still active, still involved, a burden to no one.) Her great-grandmother had lived to be over a hundred, and when she dropped dead, the *dust from the path was still on her feet.*

When the two women reached home the *Imam* was there having coffee. The women filled the *zir* in front of their doors with the water then showed the papers to Mansur and Khalil who handed them to the *Imam*.

A wide courtyard separated the three houses. There was the house where their in-laws lived; there was the house where Khalil and Zareefeh and their children lived; there was the house where Mansur, Hasna and the boys lived.

Hasna and Zareefeh brought out low threshed-bottom stools for everyone to sit on while the *Imam* read the papers that had fallen *like rain from the sky.*

Hasna listened while one-year-old Jameel and not-quite-three-year old Kareem played at her feet. Zareefeh had her infant daughter, Miriam in her lap. The older children sat on the stone floor of the courtyard expectantly waiting to hear what was written on the paper.

"It is written here that you, the *fellaheen,* are the ones who suffer most because of the strike. It is written here, that if you, the peasants, continue to support the *rebellion* – to join the rebel bands like *The Black Hand* – that your taxes will be raised, that your homes will be searched; that the men will be arrested and detained, and your women and children left destitute and unprotected."

The *Imam* added, looking meaningfully around the group: "It advises you to *stop* the rebellion, to turn in any weapon you have hidden, to listen to the village *mukhtars,* to cease in any resistance. If you do not, the authorities *threaten* that you will suffer more."

Eight-year-old Abdallah sat cross-legged at Mansur's feet. "They're afraid of us, aren't they, *Yaba?*" he said.

Mansur ruffled the raven curls on Abdallah's head and smiled. "Yes, they are afraid. They thought that we would be easy to control because we are poor and ignorant. They are surprised that we resist. They think that if they *threaten us* we will do as they wish. They do not realize that the *more* they threaten, the *more* we will resist."

Mansur paused. "You would think that they, being educated men, being British, would realize that repression only makes our support of the rebels stronger."

The popularity of the rebel bands like *The Black Hand* increased. There was more vandalism of settler trees; men were trained in the use of the firearms they had hidden; ammunition was supplied to the *fellaheen* fighters; men – like the stranger they had first seen in the coffeehouse – instructed them in the making of Molotov cocktails. The union of British colonialism with Jewish encroachment had given birth to armed insurrection.

The leaders of the rebel bands became folk heroes. Every area seemed to have its guerrilla leader: Nazareth, Hebron, Jenin, Tulkarem, and Jerusalem. Almost magical stories were woven about their exploits. There was Aref Abul Razzik of the area south of Tulkarem; while being chased by British soldiers, he would gallop away astride his white mare and *vanish* into thin air – or so the tale was told.

Many Arab men in the cities were *persuaded* to no longer wear the red Turkish fez, but to adopt the *kuffiyeh* of the peasant. The wearing of the *kuffiyeh* became a symbol of an imposed national unity between the *fellaheen* and the *med'da'knee'ya* – at least in the form of head gear.

Alongside, yet directly opposite to the rebel bands, grew the Peace Bands (*fasa'il al Salam*). The British were marginally successful in recruiting some Arab peasants to fight against the rebel bands. For the most part they were landless, poor, disgruntled with the way things were. They would do almost anything if they were paid: spy on their neighbors, work for the occupiers, and fight for the interests of absentee landowners and those rural *mukhtars* who wanted to maintain the power and influence that collaboration with the British Mandate gave them.

Mansur was invigorated by the conflict. Hasna's initial reservations and fears were replaced by tacit acceptance and support; acceptance of the situation, unwavering support of Mansur.

She loved the evenings when it was warm enough to leave the shutters on one window open so moonlight could slip between the bars and play across the faces of her sleeping sons. Kareem had been moved to the pallet where Khalil slept; Omar and Abdallah slept together, and the baby Jameel slept in the metal cradle beside the pallet of Mansur and Hasna. She would place her head on Mansur's chest and listen to the steady beats of his heart.

"I'm so glad that I have you and the children," Hasna whispered. "I'm not afraid when you are here. I know that you will always protect me and care for me. May God forgive me for how much I love you," she sighed.

Mansur laughed as he tightened his arm around her, kissing the red curls that crowned her head. "You know, you are the best wife a man could have. I have been richly blessed by Allah."

"Even though I have red hair, blue eyes and freckles?" Hasna teased.

"*Especially* because you have red hair, blue eyes and freckles," he answered. "There is no one else who can compare to you. You are a rare *beauty, habeeptee*. As I told you the night of our wedding, you are a wife fit for the Prophet himself, peace and blessing upon him."

Hasna fell asleep with her head resting on Mansur's chest. He, too, soon slept with his chin resting against Hasna's head. The moonlight continued to play across the faces of the sleeping children. The figure that had been watching through the open window silently crept away.

Chapter 19

Doberman pinschers had been imported from South Africa to *beef-up* the investigation centers. It was thought, by some within the Mandate government, that the best way to deal with the insurrection was severe *intimidation.* What better way to *intimidate* an ignorant prisoner than to have a snarling, drooling, jaw-snapping Doberman pinscher growling at him and only held back by a leash and the whim of the dog handler?

Investigation centers (called Tegart Centers after Sir Charles Tegart) began to dot the landscape. In these centers interrogators were trained in torture. Prisoners were routinely beaten, had the soles of their feet whipped, were given electric shock treatments to their genitals, and were sometimes *de-nailed.* It was found that sometimes just the *threat* of the removal of a fingernail or toenail brought the desired confession. It was *gratifying* to recognize the effect that a pair of needle-nose pliers and a slobbering Doberman could have.

Another effective technique, especially for very *mulish* detainees was a technique called *water boarding.* An especially obstinate prisoner would have his arms and legs tied to a board. A cloth bag was placed over his head and water was poured over the bag. The prisoner couldn't catch his breath; his lungs felt like they were bursting; and he had the impression that he was drowning. It was found to be *relatively* effective in the case of particularly *tenacious* prisoners.

Some within the Mandate Authority felt that the Palestinian police force and the British Army needed to have an *auxiliary* police force. It was decided to form armed *Jewish* units which would be equipped with armored vehicles and would be *on-call* when needed.

Every conceivable attempt was made to control the uprising. To prevent the threat of Arab snipers, army vehicles routinely would have an Arab peasant forced to sit on the hood of the truck. He wasn't *tied* to the truck's bonnet, but had to manage to *stay* on while the truck careened down a street. Sometimes, just for fun, the driver would suddenly brake, and the Arab riding the hood would be propelled into the street. Occasionally, he was even run-over by the truck. Another Arab would be forced to ride in the bed of the truck, sometimes when the vehicle was suddenly stopped, he would fall out, and when the driver backed-up and changed gears, he was run over.

In spite of Doberman pinchers, de-nailing, water boarding, and being shot off the hood of a moving vehicle, the armed insurrection continued. Nothing seemed to be working.

The stranger, with the piercing black eyes and bristly beard and moustache, made frequent visits to the coffeehouse. When asked his name, all he would say was: *Call me Abu Ali.*

"Is that your real name?" Mansur asked.

"It is the name I want you to know me by," the stranger smiled.

He managed to recruit a few of the young men. Mansur and Khalil were among them.

Razik sat and watched. He drank a third glass of tea. He was well into his second youth; he had passed the time when most boys marry and start families of their own; he hadn't been able to afford to get married. His father was dead and he lived with his widowed mother eking out a living by sometimes helping with a harvest, sometimes picking olives, sometimes digging gardens for people in the city. Due to the continuing strike, it had been difficult for him to find work in the city. Yet, somehow, he seemed to have money.

He listened to what the stranger said. He noted who was especially *interested* in the stranger's words. *Mansur and Khalil were interested, but of course, they would be,* he thought. *They are both younger than I am, yet they are married and have children. Mansur's wife is particularly pretty with her fair complexion, red hair and blue eyes.*

He motioned to the waiter and ordered three cups of Turkish coffee. When they were delivered to the table where the stranger, Mansur and Khalil sat, the waiter whispered to Khalil that Razik had sent them over. Mansur looked questioningly at Razik and mouthed *shukran-* thank you. Razik half-smiled, touched his hand to his heart, and nodded to Mansur.

After the stranger left, Mansur and his brother walked over to the table where Razik sat.

"Thank you for the coffee, but you really shouldn't have." Khalil said.

"It was my pleasure. And you are most welcome." Razik replied.

"What do you think of what Abu Ali has been saying?" Mansur asked.

"I think we should take to heart his words. We should work to throw off the yoke of these British dogs and their Jewish *bitches*. We should not be under the thumb of these colonialists and foreign immigrants." Razik answered.

"Are you going to join the band?" Khalil asked.

"I am thinking about it. All that really prevents me is my elderly mother. She has no one to care for her. If something should happen to me...well, who knows what would happen to her. "

Razik paused then continued. "Unlike you two, you have siblings who can care for your parents. You have parents who can care for your wives and children if something, God forbid, should happen to you. Your wives, *illhumdillah,* have brothers as well who would look out for them. You are most blessed when you think about it. There is risk, of course, but at least your families can rely on others, my mother has no one. I must think very carefully before joining the rebels, even though I would *dearly* love to."

"It is getting late. We should be going," Mansur said resting his hand on Khalil's shoulder.

"*Tis'bah ala kheir,*" they said to Razik. "Goodnight and thank you again for the coffee."

"*Entu min ah'low,*" Razik replied "You are most welcome."

Razik watched as they left the coffee shop. He waved to the waiter again. "Another glass of tea, if you don't mind," he said.

As he sipped the scalding liquid, and gingerly held the small glass in his hand, he smiled to himself. *I gave a pretty good performance, even if I do have to say so myself. It is good that I have an elderly mother whom I can use as an excuse.*

As Mansur and Khalil walked back to their compound they thought about the conversation they had had with Razik.

"Razik is not someone whom I would trust," Khalil said. "Imagine using the excuse of an *elderly mother.*"

"He *is* all his mother has. She has no siblings, no nephews or nieces, no one to care for her if something should happen to him. He is right about that," Mansur added.

"I know, but *we* also have responsibilities. *We* also have others who rely on us – who depend on us. What would happen to Hasna or Zareefeh if something should happen to us? Oh, our parents would take care of our children, but you know that Hasna and Zareefeh would be sent back to the homes of their brothers. Mother and Father would want them to remarry; they are still young. No one would take them in marriage if they had another man's children to rear. We don't have younger brothers who could marry them and take over the rearing of our children. They would have to be sent back – sent back for their own good."

"That is the one thought that makes me even hesitate to join the rebels." Mansur said. "I have expressed my fears to Hasna. At first, she had the same fears and was afraid that she would be left without a husband and without her children if something, *God forbid,* should happen to me. But she has changed her mind – not that she is not afraid of the possibility, but she says that we must have faith in God – that what is written for me – for her – for us will be the *right thing.*"

Mansur chuckled, "I would like to see anyone trying to force Hasna to return to Awad's house and to give up her children. She has a stubbornness that goes with that red hair! If I was a betting man, I would lay any money I had on Hasna."

"She and Zareefeh are allies. If Zareefeh saw Hasna taking a stand, she would be right beside her," Khalil said as he also began to chuckle. "You remember how Hasna was when we were going to plow the field without a mule; how she insisted that *we* both pull the plow while *she* pushed! My money would be on Hasna too!"

Mansur laughed. "I can still hear her asking us: *Who was the mule, and who was the plowman?* It is because we love our families that we believe we must fight. *They* are our excuse for becoming guerrillas," Mansur soberly said.

An unexpected rain began to fall as the brothers reached the compound. It wasn't really the season of the rains, yet it was raining. The shutters on the windows were already closed. There was no moonlight to slip through the bars and play across the faces of their children. The clouds hid the stars.

That night as Hasna and Mansur lay in each others' arms, Hasna said, "*Subhan Allah* that we have a night of rain this time of year. I love hearing the rain hit against the shutters and dance upon the roof. "

Under the fig tree in the yard a man stood. He looked at the shuttered window. *There will be another night,* he thought.

Chapter 20

Archibald Ashton, (Archie to his friends), tapped his Irish blackthorn baton (shillelagh) against the leg of his khaki breeches. He had served in the *Black and Tan* brigade suppressing the Irish Rebellion, and was proud of it. He was in his fortieth year, and had been recruited to serve in the British section of the Palestinian police. *Another rebellion to be put down,* he thought.

The pay was relatively good; gave him a chance to see *a bit of the world* he mused – *though he couldn't imagine squabbling over this piece of barren land with its ignorant inhabitants.* He really believed that these *backward, uneducated* people should be thanking the British for being here– bringing some order – taking them under *'their wing'* in a manner of speaking. *They shouldn't want to be rebelling against us; they should be kissing our feet in gratitude that we came.*

Of course, the British are superior to this inferior lot, he reflected. *Control is achieved through force – sometimes cracking a few heads is in order. Rebels need to be **shown** who is in power;* he reasoned punctuating his thoughts with the rhythmic beating of his shillelagh against his leg.

He had just read the British Emergency Regulations that had been issued: six years for the possession of a revolver; five years of hard labor for possessing *12* bullets! *That's my favorite,* he chuckled. Eight months in detention for the misdirecting of a detachment of British soldiers; five years for *trying* to buy ammunition from a soldier, and two weeks of jail time for possessing a *stick! That one is another favorite,* he smiled. *We'll soon show this lot who's boss!*

Archibald Ashton was a racist and a bigot. He hated Arabs and was thankful he was British.

Hasna opened the shutters and let the cool – almost cold – summer breeze that blew off the hills, slip around the bars of the windows, and perfume the one-room dwelling with the scent of jasmine, lemon, and good, clean earth. *Yes, the rocks and the earth do have a smell,* she thought.

She loved the early morning when the cloak of night had been thrown off, when Allah had painted the heavens with broad splashes of red and gold. There was certainly a rugged beauty about this land. *I can't imagine living any place else,* she thought.

At the top of the opposite hill, Rachel Rosenberg had also gotten up early. Three-year-old Samuel was still sleeping; she ran her hand over his blonde curls and sighed. She had almost *lost* him. She could still recall the panic she felt when she had turned around and found he had wandered off. She had been hysterical, running over the stony ground, screaming his name. She had finally spied him half way down the hillside. There was an Arab peasant woman ascending the hill and also trying to reach him. The woman got to him first and took him in her lap. When Rachel had finally descended the hill, Samuel had stopped crying and was sitting in the woman's lap.

Rachel recalled how grateful she felt that he was safe. She tried to *tell* the woman, but of course they couldn't understand each other. The woman had even *kissed* Samuel's shoulder, patted his back and smiled. When she was telling her husband, Moshe, about it that evening she said: "The startling thing was, Moshe, she had red hair, blue eyes and freckles; she didn't look like an Arab at all!"

Moshe was a member of the auxiliary police force that the Mandate government had recruited from Zionist settlers. He was happy to have employment; felt proud of being in this quasi-military unit (they had been issued rifles and were often called on to participate in incursions into Arab-Palestinian villages when arrests were made); began to feel more and more that *this* was *rightfully* the Jewish homeland. Sometimes at night he would dream of a homeland free of Arabs and British – a completely *Jewish homeland* – the land that God had promised them.

It was just at dusk when they came. The road into the village was blocked at both ends with military trucks. A dozen or more men, some wearing the black breeches, drill-khaki tunics, leather jackboots, and Cossack-like kolpac hats of the Palestinian-British police; some wearing the beige tunics and shorts of the auxiliary police, *all* armed with rifles jumped from the trucks.

Hasna was just hanging the straw mat, on which their evening meal had been spread, on the wall when she heard the staccato beating of rifle butts on the wooden door and the shouts of: *If'ta bab!* The children stared at the door in fright and the baby began to cry.

Mansur went to the door. As soon as he had lifted the iron hook that kept the door latched, six policemen burst into the house and forced him against the wall.

"Where are your papers? *Yallah,* give me your papers!"

Mansur reached into the cloth sash around his waist and drew out his identity papers.

Hasna, holding the baby, stood with Abdallah on one side of her and Omar on the other. Khalil and Kareem both shivered behind her holding tightly to her skirt.

"Where is your rifle?"

"There is no rifle here," Mansur answered.

"Search!" the policeman instructed the men who were with them. They looked, pulling the pallets out of the niche in the wall; they looked, thrusting long poles down into the storage bins; they looked breaking open Hasna's bridal chest spilling the contents on the floor; they looked, but they found no rifle.

"You are coming with us," the policeman said, shoving Mansur out the door and into the courtyard.

"Hold him," he barked to two of the auxiliary policemen who had accompanied them. Moshe Rosenberg took Mansur's hands and tied them behind his back. He then grabbed his arm with an iron fist.

Hasna had followed Mansur out of the house, three little boys trailing after her, the baby in her arms.

"Please, where are you taking my husband?" she asked the young man who was holding his arm.

Moshe just looked at her. He said nothing. As he stared at her, he noticed her *red hair, blue eyes and freckles! This must be the woman who rescued Samuel,* he thought. *It is unfortunate that her husband's name is on the list.*

Khalil was also in the courtyard. He, too, had his hands bound behind his back. Zareefeh and their children, along with Mansur's parents, were pleading with the policemen.

Their homes had been searched, along with the *qa'albayt* at Mansur's parents where the sheep, goats and donkey were penned, where the hens made their nests. No rifles had been found. Omar looked at the policemen as they came out of the *qa'albayt* empty handed. The rifles had been carefully hidden. He was glad that the policemen didn't think that a six-year-old would know where the guns were buried.

The men, along with four others from the village, were loaded into the trucks and blindfolded.

Abu Mansur saw the other two men who had been pushed into the truck. He knew them. He knew that they had also listened to the words of the rebel leader, Abu Ali. He *knew* that there was a spy in the village – how else would the police know *exactly* whom to arrest? *This spy must be routed out and killed,* he said to himself.

Hasna had finally gotten the boys settled for the night. She had moved the two pallets upon which they slept close together so that they were touching. She also moved the pallet that she shared with Mansur close to their pallets, taking the baby, Jameel, into bed with her. She had left one of the windows un-shuttered so that she could see the stars, so that a bit of moonlight would illumine the room. She prayed for Mansur, for Khalil, for the other two men who had been taken. She prayed that Allah would care for them and give them *strength* to endure. She prayed that Allah would give her courage and patience, that Allah would give her the stamina to care for her five sons – to be a wife of whom Mansur would be proud.

Beneath a tree, shielded by its branches, the man looked at the un-shuttered window. He silently crept toward it. If he stood on his toes, his eyes would just clear the lower ledge of the window. There was just enough moonlight for him to make out the figures of Hasna and her sons. He glanced at the sleeping figures, but his eyes came back to rest on Hasna.

She is such an unusual beauty, he thought. *She has no husband or brother-in-law to protect her. I am glad that I turned in their names,* he smiled.

In the distance a wolf howled at the moon. A brother wolf took up the cry, and it too bayed at the moon. Hasna had awakened at the sound of the wolves. She had also *felt* that she was being *watched.* She went to the opened window and looked out. She scanned the darkness. There was no one there.

The man had flattened himself against the stone wall at the side of the window. He could see Hasna through the crevice where the shutter met the wall, but she could not see him. He felt a familiar stirring between his legs. Again he smiled. *It won't be long, Hasna,* he thought to himself.

Chapter 21

"I can't shit in a bucket," Khalil whispered to Mansur. "But I can't hold it in any longer!"

"I'll stand in front of you and shield you with my body."

Khalil positioned himself over the half-filled galvanized bucket. He felt his stomach turn as he looked down at the feces swimming in urine. The nauseating odor assaulted his nostrils. He lifted the skirt of his *umbaz* and lowered his cotton trousers. He hunkered over the bucket and grunted. He was relieved. He was ashamed. He was humiliated. He looked around for a *breek* of water with which to cleanse himself. There was none.

He, Mansur, Saed and Abdel Rahman had been shoved into a cell with fifteen other men. There was no window. There were dirty straw pallets on the floor along the walls. There was a small, barred window in the door. There was a bucket.

All of the men were *fellaheen* - peasants like them. All of them, according to the stories they told, had been arrested and accused of possessing arms and of being members of rebel bands. In each case, at least according to what the men said, no weapons had been found.

"I wonder how long they will keep us." Khalil asked.

"They will keep us for as long as they want," a bearded man answered. "I have already been here for over three weeks."

"Or until they get a confession," piped in another man.

"Or until we show them where we have hidden our rifles," added a third looking at each of the others with hooded-eyes.

"Show them where any rifles are hidden and they *hang you!*" said an older man with white in his beard.

"I've heard that they have *ways* of making you talk," volunteered a youth who was trying to keep the quiver out of his voice. He was the youngest among them. Except for a few scraggly hairs on his chin, and the shadow of a moustache on his upper lip, he wasn't old enough to shave.

An older man sat on a straw pallet next to the one on which Mansur and Khalil sat. His beard and moustache were heavily threaded with gray. His *umbaz* was stained and patched. Mansur noticed his hands. Large prominent veins stood out on their backs; some of his fingernails were broken; there were dark crescents under each nail. They were the hands of a man who worked the land. They were peasant hands.

He looked at Mansur and Khalil and introduced himself. "I am Abu Waleed. Be careful what you say here," he said in an undertone. "There may be spies among us. And if not, one may say things he has heard when the pain gets too bad. It is best to say nothing that can be repeated." He nodded meaningfully in the direction of the youth.

Hasna thought that she hadn't slept, but she had. She had had a strange dream. She never remembered her dreams – in fact, she used to joke with Mansur that *she never dreamt.* Last night, or perhaps it was the early hours of the morning just before dawn, she had dreamed and she *remembered* it. She *didn't* understand it, but she could recall even the tiniest detail – she could describe the color of the dress the woman wore and almost *smell* the burning.

In the dream there was a large castle, *what the ruins of an old Crusader castle she had once seen in a village must have looked like when it was newly built,* she thought. There was a young woman standing on the ramparts of the castle. She wore a long pale gray dress; her hair was loose and fell below her hips. There were four little children huddled around her. Black smoke rose above the ramparts, flames lapped at a wooden door. She was there, alone with the children. One could *taste* her fear.

Suddenly a man appeared. It was obvious that the woman didn't know the man. She placed the four children behind her. The man advanced. He was smiling, but it wasn't a *nice* smile. He loosened the belt around his waist. The young woman could see his arousal. He advanced slowly...surely. She didn't wait. She rushed forward with out-stretched hands. She lowered her head and battered him in the stomach; with arms of steel she pushed the stunned man *over* the wall. She heard his scream and the sound of his body as it crashed against the rocks.

Sweat poured off the woman's face and dampened her red hair. Her breath came in gasps. She turned to look at the frightened faces of the children. She said to the children, "There is nothing to fear. I am here. I will take care of you."

Hasna had abruptly awakened. The woman in the dream had red hair, blue eyes and freckles. It was as though Hasna was looking – back through time – in a mirror!

The cell door opened and two burly policemen came in. They scanned the faces of each man in the room before pointing to the youth. *"Enta, ya kalb," (You, you dog)* come with us!"

The boy's eyes darted around at the faces of the other prisoners. He swallowed nervously and wet his lips. The fear in his eyes bordered on panic. He was trying not to cry.

The two burly guards dragged him out.

"Allah *ma'ak yabnee,"* Mansur called after him, *"God be with you my son,"* though he was not old enough to be the boy's father. "Allah *ma'ak."*

He was gone for over an hour. The thick walls and heavy door did not block out his screams. The screaming seemed to go on and on and on. Finally there was quiet.

The other prisoners were silent as they waited for the door to open, for the next man to be taken.

The cell door creaked open. The two burly guards dragged in the limp body of the boy. When the guards left, the other prisoners rushed over to the boy. He was barely recognizable. His eyes were swollen shut; the bruising on his cheeks were purple splotches; his *umbaz* was undone and his white cotton trousers torn and damp with urine. There were burn marks around his genitals and on his penis.

"They've burned him with cigarettes," Mansur said in a shocked voice.

Mansur lifted the boys' hands; *four fingernails had been ripped off!*

Thankfully, the youth was unconscious. Mansur sat on the pallet beside the youth and cushioned his head in his lap. Khalil had folded the pieces of the youth's torn trousers together as best he could and closed the youth's *umbaz*. The old man had torn the bottom part off the legs of his own cotton trousers and bound the youth's wounded hands. There were tears of anger in his eyes.

It was well into the night when the youth awoke. He could barely open his eyes. Through the swollen slits he looked at Mansur. "I didn't tell them anything," he mumbled through bloodied, swollen lips. "Believe me, I didn't tell them anything."

"I know *ibnee;* I know, my son. You were a man!" The youth turned his head and muffled his sobs in Mansur's lap. Mansur stroked his hair until the sobs finally stopped and the youth fell into an exhausted sleep. Mansur's own tears rolled off his cheeks. In the darkness no one saw.

Among the 20,000 *additional* British troops brought into Palestine to *subdue the rebel bands* and *put down the revolt*, was a thirty-three year old Scottish Intelligence Officer. A little eccentric but a military genius, he was chosen for the position as he was a fluent speaker of Arabic having done a tour of duty in the Sudan. Due to being raised in a very conservative family that believed in the revocable, Old Testament Biblical right of the Jews to a homeland in Palestine, and having suffered as an *underdog* of sorts while at school, he came with some strong preconceived convictions that Zionism was the answer to the problems in Palestine, that the Jews were the *underdog* and that they deserved the world's sympathy. He was convinced that they were entitled to the biblical homeland of Palestine and that he was destined to be their advocate.

After arriving in Palestine and seeing the Arab regimes of neighboring countries, he was sure that they cared little for the Arabs of Palestine, and that the Palestinian Arabs were really not oppressed – not the *underdog* – as much as the Jews were. Though he had come to work for the British Mandate, he began to work on forming a Zionist military. Orde Charles Wingate was to have a profound effect on the history of Palestine.

Abu Mansur was determined to find out who had turned in the names of his sons. He *knew* it had to be someone who knew the boys, who had seen them talking to Abu Ali, who knew where Mansur and Khalil lived, and who had something to gain.

He went to the coffeehouse that evening. He looked at the men who were sitting there drinking tea, playing backgammon, smoking water pipes. All the men had asked about Mansur and Khalil, one man in particular, Razik, had been especially *interested*.

Razik had come over and sat at the same round table. Razik had paid for a round of tea.

"I am so sorry that Mansur and Khalil were arrested," he said. "If there is anything I can do to help, I am ready. You only need but ask," he smiled placing his hand over his heart. "They are like my brothers."

"I wonder how the police knew to take *only* Mansur, Khalil, Saed, and Abdel Rahman." Abu Mansur questioned. "Surely, there are also other men who heard the stranger's words and took them to heart?" He took a sip of the sweetened tea.

"I wonder how the gendarmes knew to come to only four houses?" he paused and took another drink of tea making an appropriate slurping sound. "It would seem as though someone must have told them." He looked intently at Razik.

"*Ya, Ammo,* who can guess how those British dogs think?" He, too, took a drink of his tea, swilling it between his lips. "There is no one here who would say anything to the British authorities. *We are all one hand.*"

"Thank you for the tea. *Salam aleikum,*" Abu Mansur waved as he stalked out of the room.

I don't trust Razik, he thought as he walked up the winding path to his courtyard. *I don't trust him at all.*

That night, once again, the man waited beneath the fig tree and gazed intently at the house. Though there was a full moon, though the sky was brilliant with stars, and there was a cool breeze blowing, the shutter on Hasna's window was closed.

Chapter 22

Omar and Abdallah scooped up the dung from the sheep, goats and donkey; carefully dropping it into the *quffeh,* being sure that a little straw clung to the warm manure. They would spread it out to dry, enough distance from the house so that the smell would be carried *away* from the open windows. When sufficiently dry and hard, the manure was used as a cheap, readily available fuel. Oh, they still went with their mother to gather brush, but she used the dung-cakes to heat water for the wash, for their weekly baths, and occasionally for cooking when she cooked outside.

They were now old enough to take the sheep and goats to the hills to graze, and to milk the goats when they brought them back in the late afternoon. Hasna had taught them to rub their hands together to make them *warm* before wrapping them around a goat's teat. They would rest their curly heads against a goat's side and squeeze. The milk would squirt and splash into the tin pitcher as they squeezed. Sometimes a stray kitten would sit expectantly – waiting for a squirt of warm goat's milk. The boys would look to see if Hasna was around before trying to hit the kitten's mouth. They liked to watch the kitten dance and box the air with her paws trying to *catch* the stream of warm milk. It was a game. One time their mother had caught them squirting a teat-full of milk into a gray kitten's mouth and scolded them for wasting milk. *Milk was for making leban and lebaneh; milk was for making kishek; milk was for growing boys to drink – milk was NOT for little gray kittens,* she had said.

Hasna watched as they drove the small flock of sheep and goats out of the low-walled courtyard. The old black-and-white goat led the scraggly line. Her almost-fully-grown kid nudged her cloth-covered udder in disappointment. Hasna had decided the kid was now too big to continue to nurse and had tied a coarse-linen sack about her udder. The milk was needed for other things, not for a kid big enough to graze like the other goats and sheep. Abdallah and Omar marshaled the flock into the dirt path and up toward the rocky hills. Little four-year-old Khalil followed, waving a stick and calling to the goats and sheep: *"Yallah. Yallah. Imshee!"* He turned at the bend in the path to smile and wave at Hasna who stood at the gate holding Jameel, his brother Kareem clinging to her skirt and waving.

Mansur and Khalil, along with the other two men taken from the village, had been gone for two weeks. There had been no word from them or about them. Abu Mansur had tried to make inquires, but did not know who to ask. He had gone to the police station in Jerusalem, and they said they *knew nothing* and rudely dismissed him, saying: *Yallah. Imshee – just like his grandson, Khalil, said to the sheep and goats,* he thought.

He had also been making *quiet* inquires about Razik. The men in the village whom he asked knew Razik, but no one really *knew* him. They did know that he lived with his aged mother. They did know that he had no siblings, and that he was unmarried – long beyond the time when a man *should* be married. They did know that he never appeared to work, yet *he seemed to,* at least quite recently, *have money* to spend in the coffeehouse. They *remembered* him being present at the coffeehouse when the stranger, Abu Ali, was there – but then, *so were they* and a dozen other men.

Even quiet, *just-between-you-and-me* inquires become known. Once words are spoken, once they are drifting through the air, they will eventually be carried to the ear of the person who is being asked about.

As Abu Mansur walked down the dusty path toward his courtyard, he saw at the end of the path, just before his gate, Razik waiting for him.

"Salam aleikum, Ammie," Razik said.

"Aleikum salam," Abu Mansur answered.

Abu Mansur did not invite Razik in. *"Bid'duck ishee?"* Abu Mansur asked. Do you want something?

"I understand that you have been asking questions about me, Ammie."

Abu Mansur paused before answering. "That is right, Ammie." That was all he said.

"Why?"

"I am curious about you, Ammie."

"Curious about what?" Razik asked.

"Just curious."

"If you have any questions about me, you only need to ask. There is no need to ask others about me," Razik said, veiled anger in his voice.

"That is good to know, Ammie," Abu Mansur smiled, the smile not reaching his eyes.

"I am curious why the policemen arrested my sons." Abu Mansur said looking directly into Razik's eyes. "I think *you* had something to do with this. And when I find out..."Abu Mansur didn't finish the sentence but drew a quick line with his finger across his throat.

"*Salam aleikum,*" he said as he turned and left Razik standing in the path.

Razik watched the retreating figure of Abu Mansur and muttered a curse under his breath. *I will show him,* he thought. *I will show him in a way that he will never forget.* Just then Hasna came out of the door of her house to toss an enamel dish-pan of water onto the threshold. Her head was uncovered; her red braids swayed beyond her breasts, almost touching the warm, wet stones as she swished the water in front of the door.

Razik was obsessed with Hasna. An obsession that was hard to explain, even to himself. He had only seen her from a distance. He had never spoken to her. He hated Mansur, though there was no justifiable reason. He rationalized that Mansur had everything that *he* didn't have: friends, sons, and an exotic-looking wife. He had watched Mansur and his brother at the coffeehouse. He had seen how they were *liked* by everyone; they always had someone to sit with, play backgammon with, *talk with.* While *he,* Razik, always sat alone; no one ever invited *him* to join them.

His mother had tried to find him a bride, but none of the families she asked would give him one of their daughters. They never directly said why, but Razik *knew* they thought he wasn't *good* enough. Well, he would show them too. What wasn't freely given would be forcefully *taken.* He had fixated on Mansur's wife, Hasna –*blessing* - he had learned from his mother that that was the girl's name. His mother had made the passing comment *that the girl had red hair and blue eyes – about how unusual that was.* She would *bless* his life alright! He was different, and he *deserved* someone who was also different.

In his mind he could see the *pleasure* on her face when he mounted her.

Razik felt the familiar stirring. He smiled to himself as he thought *just how he would show Abu Mansur!* He would *show* them all.

There were still scars of the beating the youth Ibrahim had taken. The places where he had been burned with cigarettes had blistered, scabbed over, and left scars about his genitals. The bruises on his face, though still evident, had faded. There were permanent dark circles under each eye. His eyes were no longer swollen shut.

His hands were still quite sore. The fingers with the missing nails still looked as though they had been dipped in red paint. It was painful to bend his hand. He still had to be assisted when he ate, as he could not grip a spoon or hold a cup.

The group of fifteen prisoners had *adopted* him. This was especially true of Mansur, Khalil, and the old man who had bound up his wounded hands with the torn pieces of his cotton trousers.

In the two weeks they had been confined, each man had been interrogated. They had agreed among themselves that they would say *nothing;* that they wouldn't *utter* one word; that they would endure whatever they had to endure – *in silence.*

It had not been too difficult to do when they were slapped and hit. It had been a bit harder when the jailers used the old Turkish practice of whipping the bare feet of prisoners. The men had *moaned* when cigarettes were put out on their arms or on the back of their hands. They had sweated a bit when the Doberman pinschers had been brought into the room and snarled and slobbered as they strained at the leashes.

They were deaf to the curses of the interrogators; they were deaf to the references to *their manhood;* they were deaf to the insinuations about their mothers, their wives, their daughters. They grimly kept *silent* no matter what was asked, or said, or done.

The investigators were angry at the stubbornness of these men. They had thought that by torturing the young man, the others would be cowed into confessing anything. It had had the opposite effect. The torturing of the youth, Ibrahim, had made the men resolute and *bitter.*

Mansur and Khalil had taken to sleeping on either side of Ibrahim. The old man had placed his pallet at the foot of Ibrahim's bed so that he was completely surrounded. Mansur and Khalil slept with their backs toward Ibrahim, but close enough that no matter which side he turned, or where he stretched his feet, Ibrahim could feel a body next to him and know that he wasn't alone.

Razik had been unable to find a way of getting Hasna alone. She was always in the family courtyard. She was never by herself. Every night he had hidden under the branches of the fig tree beneath her window and waited. Every night the shutters were closed. He dreamt of what he would *do* to Hasna. *He knew Hasna would like it!* He dreamt of how it would bring shame to Mansur and Abu Mansur. *He would show them. He would show them! If he didn't do it tonight, then he would do it tomorrow night; if not then, then the night after. He would catch her alone. He just had to wait.*

As Razik crept beneath the branches of the fig tree and prepared to climb over the low stone wall, he saw illumined in moonlight, *Abu Mansur!* With him were his two brothers, Abu Musa and Abu Abed.

Razik felt the sweat trickle down his back. There was a trembling in his legs. His hands began to shake and his heart was beating so fast that he thought it would burst.

The three men grabbed him and whipped the *kuffiyeh* off his head, binding his hands behind him with its black-corded *iqal.* They tied the *kuffiyeh* over his head, muffling his mouth, veiling his eyes. The three men marched him up the hillside. One man held him on each side; the third pushed him from behind.

He stumbled blindly over rocks, and would have fallen if he hadn't been held in a vise-like grip. It seemed they had been walking for hours, though of course they had not been. A hand was put against his head, forcing him to bend over.

The *kuffiyeh* was removed from his face. He blinked and could see because of the moonlight bleeding through the entrance that the four of them were in a cave. Razik was forced to his knees. His eyes darted fearfully from one face to another.

"Please..." he began to whimper. "Please..."

His eyes grew wide with fear when he saw Abu Mansur take a *sikeenee* out of his sash. It was an old knife that had belonged to Abu Mansur's father. Its blade was long and curved. It was a knife that was more ceremonial – more decorative – than useful. Abu Mansur wet his fingertip and ran it along the blade's edge. It was sharp. He smiled to see the fine line of blood it drew. He put his thumb in his mouth and sucked the line of warm blood sketched on his thumb.

Abu Musa and Abu Abed removed the sash around Razik's waist. They opened his *umbaz*. They forced him on his back, his hands still bound tightly behind him. They lowered his cotton trousers.

"No! No!" screamed Razik as he struggled and writhed on the hard dirt floor of the cave. There was no one to hear his screams. A wolf began to howl at the moon as Abu Mansur made one swift swipe with his knife.

Razik's screams were silenced with another swift cut across his throat. He died instantly, but not before he realized he was no longer a man.

Abu Mansur, Abu Musa, and Abu Abed grimly rolled Razik's body into a far corner of the cave. They silently sealed the cave's entrance with stones.

The stars twinkled in the sky; the moon illuminated their descent to the village; another wolf began to howl.

Chapter 23

Razik's disappearance caused as much impression as a sandal print on a dusty road. Men in the coffeehouse had paused in the smoking of their water pipes, or as they threw the dice in a game of backgammon, or wiped their moustache after taking a sip of hot tea, to *speculate* for a moment about his disappearance, but no one really cared. It was almost as though *he had never been.*

Abu Mansur and his two brothers felt no remorse. They felt no guilt about the cave and the secret sealed therein. They felt that they had acted honorably. The punishment had been *appropriate.* The punishment had been *just.* They had been the instruments of God.

They *had* sent their wives to visit Razik's mother. She was not responsible for the actions of her son; she was a widow, and her son had disappeared. It was only right that she be visited.

The three women went.

Razik's mother was a silent, withdrawn skeleton of a woman. She looked to be in her early sixties. The three sisters-in-law had known her as a girl; *she can't be more than forty-five,* they individually thought. Unfortunately, it seemed as though her womb had closed after the birth of Razik, as she had *swallowed no more flies.*

"I don't know where he could have gone," his mother said softly. Im Mansur, Im Musa, and Im Abed had to strain to hear what she was saying.

"He wouldn't just go away and leave me here. Something...something must have happened to him," she said dried-eyed.

She looked out the open door – not at them – and spoke as though she was speaking not to them, but to herself. "He was always such a *strange* child. I never knew what he was thinking. Sometimes...sometimes he would look at me with such *hatred.*" She stopped as though she had realized what she had said.

"He was really a good son to me; an *ideal* son really. He was always so caring about my needs." She looked directly into the eyes of the three women *daring* them to contradict her. She was really trying to convince herself that what she had said was true.

"How are you managing, Im Razik?" They asked.

"Oh, I am getting by, *illhumdillah.* I don't eat much. Allah will provide," she sighed. "If I had had a daughter, or daughter-in-law, it would have been different," she said wistfully. "But..."

As the three sisters-in-law wove their way up the dirt path to their homes they had come to a decision. Im Mansur had always had an overly compassionate heart. She had been the one that insisted that Hasna bring her nephew Abdallah with her when she married Mansur. She had been the one to convince Abu Mansur that Mansur and Khalil, now that they were married, should have houses of their own. She wasn't the typical mother-in-law.

"Though we all have large families to feed, we can surely spare two loaves of bread and a cooked meal. We daily cook and bake for our families, what is one more mouth? I am sure that our daughters-in-law will also be willing to participate in the plan. We can rotate so it is not a burden on any one household. What do you think?" Im Mansur asked her sisters-in-law.

Im Musa, who was the eldest of the three and most out-spoken, looked put-out. "I am only *mad* that the idea came from you and didn't come from *me!*"

"Why, we three and all our daughters-in-law," Im Abed said, counting on her fingers, "represent *ten* households. Ten! It can easily be done. Who cannot spare two loaves of bread and a hot meal every ten days?"

When the plan was told to Hasna, she immediately volunteered Omar and Abdallah to collect the bread and cooked food each day and to take it to Im Razik. Her mother-in-law smiled at her and agreed.

"Omar and Abdallah can take the food that you, Zareefeh and I prepare, but both Im Musa and Im Abed have grandsons the ages of Omar and Abdallah who can take the food from *their* households. This way it is not a burden on anyone."

That night the three brothers met at the coffeehouse. Over small cups of thick coffee they spoke of the plan devised by their wives.

"Is it not strange," Abu Abed said, "that it is *our* wives who have taken it upon themselves to feed Razik's mother?"

"Is it not strange," added Abu Musa, "that knowing what we know that it is *our* wives – the mother and aunts of Mansur and Khalil who are doing this generous act?"

"It *is strange,*" Mansur reflected, looking at his two brothers, "but it is all part of God's plan, *subhan Allah.* It somehow only seems *right* that Razik's mother be cared for by our households."

The three brothers sat in silence as they sipped the hot, pungent coffee. "Our mother chose well when she chose our wives. How many women would be as generous and compassionate as they?" Abu Mansur asked.

"And they chose well our daughters-in-law," Abu Abed said.

The three nodded as Abu Musa said, "We have been richly blessed."

Mansur and Khalil, along with the other prisoners who had been arrested with them, were released a month after their imprisonment. No confessions had been given or signed. As abruptly, as inexplicably, as they had been arrested they were released.

Their parting with Ibrahim was quite poignant. Ibrahim would bear some of the scars of his imprisonment for a lifetime – some visible, some invisible. He would come out of the experience knowing the *worst* of man, and also the *best* of man.

As he hugged each man in turn, he clung to Mansur just a bit longer than to the others. "I don't know how to thank you, *akhouy*- my brother, for all you have done for me. If it hadn't been for you, and Khalil, and Abu Waleed – I would not have survived. You three *saved* me."

Mansur hugged him hard and kissed him on both cheeks. "You must come and visit us in our village. You are now our *brother*. Our homes are your home." Mansur smiled as he patted him on the back. There were tears in their eyes.

"You also have a home with me, *ibnee*," Abu Waleed said. "Come, I will go back to your village with you and deliver you to your father and tell him what a brave son he has. Maybe I will ask him if I can *adopt* you," he joked. "I would be proud to have a son like you."

Omar and Abdallah had just shut the sheep and goats in the *qa'albayt* when Mansur and Khalil limped through the gate into the courtyard.

"*Yaba! Ammo!*" they cried racing barefoot across the stone courtyard flinging themselves into the outstretched arms of their father and uncle.

"*Yum'ma! Yum'ma! Yaba* is here!" Omar shouted.

The courtyard was soon filled as Zareefeh and her children, Abu and Im Mansur and their younger children ran into the courtyard. Hasna had not even taken time to cover her hair; her red braids flying as she hurried into the courtyard, Jameel in her arms, four-year-old Khalil running ahead of her, and two-year old Kareem holding tightly to her skirt.

Mansur and Khalil were overwhelmed. Mansur bent down so he could gather his four sons into his arms. Little Jameel had just learned to say *Yaba*. He struggled in Hasna's arms and kept leaning down reaching for his father.

Mansur looked up with tears in his eyes and took the struggling infant from Hasna. Jameel nestled against Mansur's shoulder and sighed as he wrapped his arms around Mansur's neck. He would raise his head and patting his father's cheeks say: *Yaba. Yaba.*

That night, as they lay together, Mansur's arms around Hasna, her head resting against his shoulder, he told her some of what had had happened in prison. He told her of the humiliation, the beatings, the whipping of their feet.

"That is why I still limp a bit," he whispered, "the soles of my feet have not completely healed."

He told her most about Ibrahim and all that had happened to him and how – in spite of all the torture – Ibrahim had told them nothing.

"I have never seen a man so beaten. I have never seen a boy so brave," Mansur said with tears in his voice. "He is my *brother.*"

Hasna held him tightly, her tears dampening the hairs on his chest. "We must go and visit him as soon as you are completely well. We must take the children and introduce them to their brave *Uncle Ibrahim.*"

"I have missed you so much," Mansur mumbled against her lips.

"And I have missed *you,*" she said and kissed him, as he gently rolled her beneath him.

Chapter 24

It was dusk and still the boys were not back with the flock. Hasna was worried. *They should have been back long before this and already have the milking done,* she thought to herself.

She went to find Mansur, juggling Jameel in her arms, Kareem firmly gripping her skirt as she moved. *She had a flash of the toddler Abdallah always within a hand's grasp of her skirt.*

She found Mansur in the courtyard talking to Khalil. They were sitting with their backs against the stone wall soaking their feet in basins of water. Their walking had improved, but their feet still bothered them from the whipping they had received in prison.

"Abdallah and Omar are not back yet," she frowned. Mansur and Khalil readily noticed the worry in her voice. "I am afraid something has happened. Little Khalil is with them as well."

Mansur and Khalil dried off their feet and slipped their sandals on. Just then Zareefeh had come out of her door. Hasna called to her and waved to her to come over.

"The boys aren't back yet with the flock. Would you mind watching Jameel and Kareem so I can go with them?" Hasna said as she passed Jameel into her arms and disengaged little Kareem's fingers from her skirt.

"Go with Amti Zareefeh, *habeebee*," she said to him as she took a fold of Zareefeh's skirt and put it into his grasping palm.

Khalil had gone to the *qa'albayt* and come back with a kerosene lantern. "It is getting dark," he said. "We may need some light."

The three of them hurriedly trudged up the dirt path, crossed a stony field, and climbed the winding path that the boys usually followed when taking the flock to graze.

When they got high enough up the slope, they began to call: "Abdallah! Omar! Abdallah! Omar!"

A crescent moon hung in the sky, casting just enough light to see the flock huddled together and a four-year old Khalil walking around them gently taping the backs of the sheep and goats with a stick to keep them together.

Mansur reached him first. "Where are Abdallah and Omar, *Yaba*?" He tried to keep the panic out of his voice.

"One of the lambs was missing and they went to search for it. They told me to stay here with the sheep and walk 'round and 'round them and softly touch their backs with the stick to keep them from wandering off."

Little Khalil tried not to cry. "They haven't come back yet. I keep calling, but no one answers."

"It's alright, *Yum'ma*," Hasna said putting a protecting arm around him. "I will stay here with you and the sheep while *Yaba* and *Ammo Khalil* find Omar and Abdallah."

The men frantically climbed further up the mountain; their voices were hoarse from calling. Finally they heard a feeble, "*Yaba,* we're here. *Yaba,* here!"

Khalil swung the lantern over the side of a precipice. They could see in the ravine below three figures: Omar, Abdallah, the lamb.

"I can't climb up, *Yaba.* Abdallah is hurt. I can't make him wake up," Omar cried.

"Stay where you are, *Yaba.* I am coming down to you."

Mansur gripped the stony outcroppings as he gingerly descended the slippery slope. His sandaled feet kept sliding. There seemed to be no sure footholds where he could lever his sore feet.

Finally he reached the boys, having slid most of the way down. Omar's face was wet with tears and he was trembling.

Mansur ran his hands over Abdallah. There was a bloody gash on his head and he was unconscious. Mansur tried to arouse him, but Abdallah would not awaken.

"Go and get Hasna. Leave the lantern so you will know where to find us. Khalil will have to stay with the sheep. You must come down and help me get the boys up," Mansur shouted at his brother.

Khalil ran back to where Hasna and the flock were, stumbling over the rocks in his path not really able to see where he was going.

"Hasna, Mansur has found the boys but Abdallah is injured. They are at the bottom of a ravine and you must come and hold the lantern so I can climb down to help get the boys up. "

He turned to Khalil, "You must be a big boy, *Ammo,* and watch the sheep by yourself for just a little longer."

There were tears in the four-year-old's eyes as he watched his mother and uncle disappear into the darkness.

Khalil knew that the quickest way down the rocky slope was to *sit* and *slide.* So that is what he did. He slid down the stony side controlling his speed by digging his sandaled feet into the dirt and grabbing onto clumps of brush as he fell.

He too examined Abdallah.

"We must get him home," Mansur said. "Put him on my back."

Mansur knelt down in the dirt and bent over. Khalil maneuvered the limp Abdallah onto his back, placing Abdallah's arms over Mansur's shoulders. Mansur gripped his arms tightly and rose to his feet.

Khalil picked up a protesting Omar. "I can climb back up, *Ammie.* Carry the lamb," he said.

A fleeting smile crossed Khalil's face. He picked up the lamb and, opening his *umbaz* just above the cloth sash, placed it securely against his chest.

"Omar, you go ahead of me, *Yaba*," Mansur instructed the six-year old.

"Khalil you climb behind me so you can push if I start to stumble and fall."

They made slow progress over the sheer, rocky surface. Khalil *did* have to brace himself and push when Mansur slipped and would have fallen back into the ravine.

Hasna leaned over the precipice as far as she could; the lantern a sliver of flame in the darkness.

Omar was the first to climb out of the ravine. He hugged his mother. She passed him the lantern as she reached down to pull Mansur and Abdallah onto the precipice.

Mansur knelt down and *rolled* Abdallah into Hasna's lap.

"*Yum'ma, Yum'ma*," Hasna cried gently slapping Abdallah's cheeks, vigorously rubbing the palms of his hands. He did not awaken.

Khalil climbed onto the precipice; the lamb still nestled in the front of his *umbaz*.

Mansur knelt and took the limp body of Abdallah into his arms. Khalil took the lantern from Omar and led their way back to the flock. Omar carried the lamb which had wandered off from its mother.

Omar and his little brother drove the flock down the hill, across the stony field, down the dirt path that led to their courtyard. Mansur and Khalil took turns carrying the unconscious Abdallah. Hasna kept a hand on Abdallah's head, stumbling over the rocks, blinking back the tears, but never losing contact with her *son*.

Abu and Im Mansur were standing at the gate when they caught sight of them. They ran down to meet them.

Abu Mansur went to take Abdallah from his son's arms, but Mansur only gripped Abdallah more firmly in his arms. "*La, Yaba. La,*" he mumbled with tears in his voice. "Go and get Awad."

There was no doctor in the village, but they sent for the aged midwife, Im Hussein – the same woman who had delivered them all; the same woman who had cared for Hasna when her father had made her fall from the fig tree.

Abdullah lay on the pallet he shared with Omar. His father, Awad, was in the room. His *"father"*, Mansur was in the room; and of course his *"mother"*, Hasna, who was really his aunt.

Im Hussein ran knowing hands over Abdallah. She examined the gash on his head. There was a gentle stream of blood flowing from the side of Abdallah's mouth. Hasna caught each dark drop with a clean rag as the tears ran unhindered over her freckles and dripped off her chin.

Im Hussein looked at Awad, at Mansur, and finally at Hasna.

"The gash on his head will heal, but I fear that there is something *broken* inside. He shouldn't be bleeding from his mouth – the blood is dark." She nodded her head sadly.

"There is nothing I can do. All you can do is to keep him comfortable. He is in the hands of Allah. *Allah yesh'feeh.*" *(May God heal him.)*

"Is he in any pain?" Mansur asked brokenly.

"No, my son. I don't think so."

Awad just stared at his son. The tears he tried to hold back making rivulets down his face, disappearing into his bristly black beard.

Abdallah seemed to be sleeping. His breathing was soft, and *almost* regular, Hasna thought as she rested a hand against his chest – just above his heart.

Zareefeh came over to Hasna and whispered that she was taking the children over to her house for the night. She carried, Jameel; Khalil carried his four-year-old nephew, and dragged a protesting Omar toward the door.

"I want to stay with my brother, *Ammie*. Let me stay with my brother," he pleaded.

Awad, Mansur, and Hasna all said at the same time, "Let him stay."

So Omar was allowed to stay and keep silent vigil with his parents and uncle.

Mansur and Awad sat on the floor next to the pallet on which Abdallah lay, leaning their backs against the un-plastered wall of the room. Omar had crawled into Mansur's lap, finally dozing off; his curly head nestled against his father's chest.

Hasna had lain down on the pallet with Abdallah. She drew his body close to hers. She was remembering him as the baby he had been, she no more than a child herself; she remembered him clinging to her skirt when he first learned to walk; she remembered him begging his father, Awad to be allowed to stay with her and Mansur; she remembered when he first called her *Yum'ma;* she remembered how she felt when Awad briefly had taken him from her. She had thought her heart would break. It was breaking now.

Mansur and Awad had finally fallen into an exhausted sleep. Omar slept in his father's arms. The morning call to prayer was just echoing over the silent hills, when Abdallah awoke. He turned to Hasna and smiled. *"Yum'ma,"* he said as he softly touched her freckled cheek. *"Yum'ma..."* Hasna held him in her arms as he slipped into heaven.

Chapter 25

For months after the accident and Abdallah's death, Hasna went through the motions of living. She still had Mansur and four little boys to care for, and as she had *suspected*, there was another baby on the way. She still had to cook and clean. She still had to gather brush, do the wash, bake bread, and help Omar with the milking. She still had to do the multitude of things which defined her day. She was in constant motion from dawn-to-dusk, and she was glad for the exhausting, *numbing* activity.

At the time of his death, she had thought that her heart would break. It didn't. She consoled herself with the belief that: *Allah doesn't give a person more than he can bear. She could bear this; she knew she could.* She wanted *desperately* to *believe* it was true.

At first it had been hard. Kareem would tug on her skirt, and for a fraction of a moment *she remembered the toddler Abdallah tugging on her skirt.* She would sling the baby, Jameel, onto her hip, and for an instant *she almost thought she was carrying the baby Abdallah on her hip.* She would raise the cotton quilt over Omar, and pass her hand through his curls, and for a second her hand trembled as it moved to smooth the curls of a head that was no longer there. It had been hard, but hearts don't break; *they may crack,* she thought, *but they don't break.*

Almost three months to the day, as Hasna lay in an exhausted sleep, she had a dream. In the dream a happy, joyous Abdallah was running toward her. His arms were reaching for her as he ran. He was smiling and calling: *Yum'ma! Yum'ma!* In the dream he *leapt* into her arms. He put his two hands on her freckled cheeks and smiled into her eyes. *I have missed you so, Yum'ma. But I am so happy here. It is a wonderful place! And do you know? I can see you and Yaba, and Omar and Khalil and Kareem and Jameel every day. I don't want you to be sad, Yum'ma. I am always with you – I am always right here,* he had said putting his hand against her heart. *And you are always right here,* he had said putting her hand on his heart. *I love you, Yum'ma, just as I know you will always love me.*

In the dream Hasna had watched as he disappeared into the mist. She was filled with a great feeling of peace. She was *confident* that he was well, that he was happy, that, yes, *he did live in her heart and that he always would.*

The next morning she shared part of the dream with Mansur. She could almost *see* a dark cloak lift from his shoulders. He smiled for the first time in months.

She went to see her brother, Awad. This past month, even though he was still in his thirties, his hair and beard had turned white. He had buried two wives, and now his only son. He had fathered no children with his current wife, Laila, and he *knew* it was his fault.

"Awad, take a walk with me," Hasna said. "There is something I want to tell you."

Awad reluctantly went with her. He had found any activity a chore. He would sit for hours doing nothing, brooding over his life – the emptiness of it, the hopelessness; he fervently wished that *he had died and not Abdallah.*

"I had a dream last night in which Abdallah came to me," Hasna started. "In the dream he was happy, *joyous* even. He said he was in a *wonderful* place and that he could *see* all of us. He said that he knew we loved him and that we *continue* to love him. He said that we were in his heart, just like he was in ours." Hasna paused and studied Awad's face.

"Do you believe that that is true?" Awad asked in a trembling voice. There were tears threatening to fall. "Do you *really* believe that he is happy and in a wonderful place? Do you *really* believe that he can still love us?"

Hasna looked steadily into his eyes. Her own eyes were clear and tearless. *"On the life of my children, I know* that the dream was true. It has been a *gift* from God. He saw my grief, and knew that I needed proof." Hasna gripped Awad's arm in a vise-like grip.

"Abdallah *loves* you, Awad. He *continues* to love you. Believe that! It is true!"

"I wasn't a good father to him," Awad said through trembling lips. "I gave my son away."

"It *was because* you loved him; you were the best father you could be at the time when you allowed Mansur and me to care for him. It takes a *good* father to put his son before himself."

"You were always a good mother to him, Hasna, even when you were only a little girl yourself," Awad said patting Hasna's shoulder.

"Thank you, Awad, for sharing your son with us," Hasna said as gentle tears spilled over and started to roll down her cheeks.

Probably for the first time in his life, Awad hugged Hasna. He clung to her for just a moment, as she clung to him. Both were remembering the little boy that bound them together more than the bonds of being brother and sister.

"Come back to the house and have a cup of tea," Awad insisted wiping the tears from his beard.

Hasna went back to the house with him. They sat on low, thresh-bottomed stools in the sun leaning their backs against the stone wall of the courtyard. The scent of jasmine perfumed the air.

Awad's wife, Laila, brought out three glasses of steaming tea. A single mint leaf floated on the surface of each glass.

The three sat and talked of unimportant things. As Hasna got up to leave, Laila said, "I'll walk to the gate with you." She slipped her arm through Hasna's.

"Thank you, *yokh'tee* (my sister). Thank you!" Awad smiled at her.

"I have a secret," Laila said shyly.

"A secret?"

"Yes, I haven't told Awad yet, but...I have finally *swallowed a fly!*"

"You're pregnant!" Hasna gasped. "I am so happy for you, *Mart Ah'khoo'ee.* Awad will be so pleased!"

As Hasna wound her way up the dirt path to her home, she thanked Allah for the gift of the dream. She could hear in her heart an excited voice call, *Yum'ma! Yum'ma. I am so happy.* She *knew* that somewhere, somehow, Abdallah was watching. *Miracles do happen,* she thought.

That afternoon when she went to help Omar with the milking of the goats, she saw that he was already there and that beside him sat four-year-old Khalil. Omar was showing him how to rub his hands together to make them warm. He was carefully showing him how to squeeze the goat's teat so that the milk would squirt into the tin. Khalil couldn't quite make it work – not even a trickle dripped into the tin.

"Your hands aren't quite strong enough yet, *habeebee,* but every day we will practice."

"Will I be as good as Abdallah?" he asked.

"Well, of course you will be as good as him," a serious Omar told him. "I'll tell you a secret, Khalil. I *saw* Abdallah last night while I slept, and he *told* me he is watching out for all of us. You know how *Yum'ma* puts her hand on our hearts and tells us that she is always there? Well, Abdallah told me the *very same thing.* He said that we are always in his heart, and that he is always in our hearts." A very adult-acting Omar ruffled Khalil's curls

"You know what else he told me?"

"What?" asked a curious Khalil looking at Omar with big black eyes.

"He said to tell Khalil, tell *you,* my brother, that you are going to be even *better* at milking goats than he was!"

Hasna, wiping the easy tears from her eyes, turned and walked back to the house.

A little later Omar and Khalil, both carrying the tin bucket of milk, came across the courtyard and into the house.

"Here's the milk, Omar proudly said. "Khalil helped me with the milking today. You don't need to help me, *Yum'ma.* I'm training Khalil to do it. And, *Yum'ma,* I know that Khalil and I can take the flock to the hills tomorrow by ourselves. You can trust us."

"You two can take the flock tomorrow by yourselves," Hasna said, "but I think that Kareem and Jameel and I will walk up to meet you when it is time to come home. If that is *alright* with you two," she laughed.

Omar went up and threw his arms around her waist. He held back the tears that threatened to spill as he mumbled into her sash, "Oh, *Yum'ma,* you got your *laughter* back!"

Hasna bent over, and hugging him to her breast, kissed his curls. "Yes, I have my laughter back, *habeebee.*"

As Hasna looked up, she *thought* she caught a glimpse of a smiling Abdallah.

"Subhan Allah. Subhan Allah," she murmured. She put her hand over her heart as she silently thanked God for the blessing of the dream – for the *assurance* that the dream had given her. She put her hand over her heart, and she *knew* – not just *believed* – but *knew that Abdallah was there.*

There *were* times though when she could not stop the tears from flowing. There *were* times, when in spite of the dream, in spite of the assurance that Abdallah was well, she challenged God's wisdom in taking him. She wished that He, in His ultimate wisdom, had seen fit to have *left* Abdallah a little longer.

Chapter 26

Increasing violence marked the years of 1937-1938. The guerrilla bands grew in number and in activity. Attacks were directed at British forces and at the growing number of Jewish settlements. Resistance, to the peasants and to a growing number of the *effendi* in the cities, seemed the *only* alternative to the Mandate and the increasing immigration of Zionists and the encroachment of their colonies.

The revolutionary spirit spread to the cities. Men in the city began wearing the peasant headdress – the *kuffiyeh* so the British police would find it more difficult to identify men from the villages. They also began to leave their identity cards at home so it would be harder to verify if a man was from the city or the country.

The Mandate colonialist government sided with the Zionist immigrants and created, trained, and armed auxiliary police bands from among them. These bands were used in the searches of Palestinian villages, and often acted as a vigilante force. The British and the increasing Jewish population linked arms in fighting a *mutual* enemy – *the Arab.*

The creation and support of a settler society was laying the foundation for a military state. The settlers felt that they had *no alternative* but to fight. The Arab Palestinians also felt that they, too, had *no alternative.*

Incidents of British and Zionist terrorism in the villages made some villages *afraid* to supply the rebels with ammunition and food; others became *empowered* and *increased* their support for the rebels.

Arab *mukhtars* were *warned* that any attacks on British forces within the *vicinity* of their villages would result in reprisals on the village – even if the perpetrators had not come from that village. It was felt that the Arab attacks should be subdued with an *iron fist.*

In 1938, a number of peasants were hanged for being in *possession* of arms; many men were imprisoned; many houses were demolished. The Mandate government deemed any means legitimate to suppress the rebellion and ultimately control the population.

The Arabs were portrayed in the British press as *bandits* while the Mandate forces were generally *praised* for their efforts in controlling the rebellion. The Arab Palestinian peasants – especially the Arab Rebel leaders were vilified. The Mandate government became convinced that the only way of controlling the situation was by force and taking decisive, often *brutal* action – however regrettable it might be at a later time.

The only final solution seemed to be the division of the country into two. The recommendation of the Peel Commission was that the fledging Jewish population be given the northern part of the country and the fertile, coastal area; and that the Arabs be given the southern and the rocky hill country. It was suggested that they become part of Transjordan.

This of course enraged the Arabs. It was into this atmosphere of increasing tension, and the possibility of transfer and division of the country, that Hasna's and Mansur's fifth child was born.

The birth of her fifth child was relatively easy for Hasna; at least as compared with the other four births. It was as though there was a *drawstring* on her womb. Once the *string* was loosened, the husky babe just *slid* out. He almost *slipped* from the midwife's hands as though he had been *already* rubbed in oil.

He had sturdy limbs and a solid, round, dimpled butt. His black hair was so long that it practically touched his heavy eyebrows. His cheeks were covered with a fine film of hair; it even looked like he had the beginning of a moustache.

Hasna had to admit that others would think he wasn't a very pretty baby but as the Arabic phrase said: *Even a monkey in his mother's eyes looks like a gazelle.* To her, the baby was beautiful.

Mansur, gazing down at his little son for the first time, laid his finger in the baby's palm. The baby immediately wrapped his long, tapering fingers around his father's.

"He has a strong grip," Mansur smiled at Hasna.

"What shall we name this little man?"

Hasna gave Mansur a loving, though exhausted smile: "We shall call this one *Imad.*"

"He *looks* like an *Imad*. He is certainly built like a stone *pillar*. Look at those arms, *ma'shallah*," Mansur said. (The name *Imad* meant a stone support for the house.)

"A house is made strong by the number of sons it has," Mansur added.

"What about the number of *daughters* it has?" Hasna joked.

"Sons *bring* daughters to a family." Mansur paused, "Especially if they have a strong mother like you; a mother who will choose just the *right* daughters-in-law." Mansur responded.

The afternoon of the birth of her fifth child, Hasna was already up preparing the evening meal. Oh, she did perhaps move a little slower, but that was to be expected. In a day or so she would have her strength back. She was young. She was strong. She was used to hard work.

She didn't know the exact date of her birth; nor did she know the exact date of Mansur's birth. She only knew that they had both been born in the spring. If her calculations were right, she was twenty-one and Mansur twenty-six.

Life is not measured in years, she thought. *It is measured in experiences.*

She had given birth five times, but all of her babies had survived and she and Mansur had been blessed with *sons*. Abdallah had died when he was about eight, but he had blessed her life all those years. Mansur had been imprisoned and beaten, but he had *survived* and come back to her. Her father had hated her and had tried to kill her, but he *hadn't* killed her and his treatment of her had made her strong and independent. She worked like a mule, but all the women she knew worked hard. And yes, she had been married off at thirteen and a half, but she had been blessed in having a husband who was young, not old and blind, and a husband who *loved* her. She had *seen* how her father had been with her mother; she had *observed* how Awad was with his wives; she had heard the whisperings at the well when the married women would sometimes talk about their husbands – yes, she was richly blessed when she thought of Mansur. She knew her life could have been *so different.*

Hasna became obstinate – '*almost irrational,'* Mansur thought - when it came to Abdallah's lamb – the lamb he had attempted to rescue and that had resulted in his death. It had been decided that the lamb, which was now fully grown, be sold for slaughter. When Hasna discovered which sheep it was, she dug her heels in and said that *it was not going to happen!*

Mansur had been surprised at the vehemence of her objection.

"Hasna, it is a ram. We already have a ram; we do not need two. We can sell it for a good price. I am selling the ram."

He was adamant.

So was Hasna.

"Sell the older ram, but leave this one," she had proposed.

"The younger sheep will bring a better price. With the older ram the meat will be tough. I am selling the younger one." And he had, unthinkingly, added, "This is really my decision, not yours."

"*Your* decision is it?" she had added; the fire-red hair lending a flame to her tongue.

"This is the sheep that Abdallah lost his life in rescuing. It is *meant* to live. Did he lose his life so that you could sell this sheep? This ram is destined to live, and live it shall!" Hasna said as she grabbed the ram by the wool behind its head and began pulling it back toward the *qa'albayt*.

Mansur stood in her way and blocked the entrance into the stable. He tried to remove Hasna's hand from the back of the ram's neck.

He grabbed her hand and then looked into her eyes. The blue eyes penetrated into his. He could see the snapping stubbornness. He could see, for the first time in the seven years they had been married – *defiance!*

It startled him. Hasna had always been so complaint. She had never, purposely *defied* him. She had never *opposed* him. He saw, out of the corner of his eye, Omar holding the hands of Khalil and Kareem looking at their parents. *I have to take a stand,* he thought, *especially in the eyes of my sons.*

"Hasna, *remove* your hand!" he ordered.

"So, now you are going to *order me!?*" Hasna said looking at him defiantly.

"You *forget* your place," Mansur hissed in a low voice.

"I *know* my place," she whispered – again looking at him with defiance. "But the ram *will not be sold.*"

It was then it happened. Without thinking, Mansur raised his hand and brought it down giving Hasna a stinging blow to her cheek.

Hasna released her grip of ram's wool. She looked long and clearly into Mansur's eyes. The tears in her eyes did not fall. The print of his hand was red among the freckles of her cheek – each finger was distinctly outlined. She straightened the worn shawl that covered her head, and abruptly turning, slowly walked back toward the house.

She stopped to say something to Omar and Khalil then took Kareem by the hand and went into the house.

Omar and Khalil stared at their father in disbelief then silently walked by him into the *qa'albayt* to do the morning milking of the goats.

Mansur couldn't believe what he had just done. Immediately when his hand made contact with her cheek he was full of regret. He knew that other men

.

sometimes struck their wives, but he wasn't that kind of man.

A few moments later Hasna came out of the house. She was carrying the metal cradle in which Imad slept in one hand. On her hip little Jameel rode; Kareem was holding tight to her skirt. She put the cradle beneath the shade of the fig tree and set Jameel on the ground beside it. She said something to Kareem and he also sat with his brothers.

Hasna went to the pile of kindling and brush at the side of the house. She sorted through it and finally found a good, sturdy stick. She tried to break it and could not. *This will do,* she thought.

She carried the stick to Mansur and handed it to him.

"You must beat me for my disobedience," she said. "I should not have shamed you in front of your sons. I had forgotten my place. I am sorry." She reached for his hand, kissed it and placed it against her head.

"*Hasna...,*" he stammered, his voice choked with emotion. "I'm not going to beat you," he said throwing the stick away from him.

Omar and Khalil had been standing in the door of the stable. They had seen what their mother had done; they had heard what their parents had said, and seen how their father had thrown the stick away.

That night after the boys had gone to sleep on their pallets, after Hasna had nursed the new baby and put him in his metal cradle next to her side of the pallet, she too lay down to sleep. For the first time in their married life she did not rest her head on Mansur's chest. She drew herself up into a ball and lay, barely touching Mansur's silent form.

"Hasna," Mansur said in a choked voice reaching for her, "Hasna, I am sorry."

Hasna was trying to control her weeping, "I, too, am sorry. I should not have defied you. I was not a very good wife today."

Mansur gently pulled her toward him. He turned her so she was facing him. He positioned her head against his shoulder.

"*This* is where you should be sleeping, *habeeptee. Here* on my shoulder."

Hasna wept against his shoulder, her tears dampening the hairs on his chest. His own tears, unseen by Hasna, ran down his cheeks into his bushy moustache.

He kissed the top of her head. "I will not sell the young ram," he whispered.

She tightened her arms around him. "But you must," she said. "You were right; the young ram will bring more money."

"I have made up my mind," he said tightening his arms around her. "The young ram will live – you were right, *it was meant to be.*"

Chapter 27

"Cut off the head and the serpent dies," British Officer Walter Webb expounded as he took the cigarette out of his mouth and tapped the ashes into the brass ash tray. He rearranged the cards in his hand. "That's what we need to do; hunt down the rebel leaders. Kill them and the rebellion is finished. A lot of these leaders are opportunists – they are in it for what they can get for themselves. There is naturally a lot of ego involved. A number of these rebel leaders think they are the *cat's meow* – when they are really just the *cat' whiskers* – if that!"

"More like the *fur ball* the cat chokes on," added red-haired Edmund Warrender. "There's no central leadership at all. They *can't* hope to succeed when there is no *ONE* person calling the shots. You have a collection of little demigods. All dressed up in their peasant garb, with a curved dagger in their belt, and a *rag on their head,"* he laughed. "I'll take one," he said, reaching for a card.

"I was talking to some of the men who used to be former members of the *Black and Tans.* They are *superior buggers* that lot– but they have the right attitude. They think these peasants are really *inferior* bastards. Look at 'em: they live in one-room houses, eat off the floor, no electricity in their hovels; no running water. Their women carry water from a well on their heads, for

Christ's sake. They're still living in Bible times. They should be kissing our feet that we are here to raise them out of the shit-hole they're livin' in." Ralph Reynolds interjected as he laid down his cards to show that he had won the hand. "Read 'em and weep. Read 'em and weep," he grinned as he raked in the coins.

"Let's play one more hand. Give me a chance to win some of my money back," Edmund said.

"Okay, just one more. It's getting late," Walter said as he glanced at his wristwatch.

"Have a big *date* tomorrow, do we?" Charlie Ashton asked, a cigarette bobbing in the corner of his mouth as he spoke. "Maybe with one of these barefoot Arab *beauties,* hey?" He laughed.

"Speaking of Arab *beauties.* We were driving through a village the other day, and My God, I swear it is true, I saw this barefoot peasant woman with *red* braids and *freckles.* The jeep drove right by her. She glanced at us for a moment as she pulled a child out of our path. And, believe it or not, she had *blue* eyes. Blue! Dress her differently and you would think you were looking at a Scottish lass from Edinburgh. She looked enough like Edmund, here, to be his bloody sister."

"I guess the Crusaders did *something more* than try to wrest the Holy Land from the *infidels.* They took time out in their sword playing, didn't they? They spread a few legs and left a *little reminder* of *heath* and *highlands!*" Edmund coarsely laughed. "I think one of my ancestors fought in the Crusades – so my mom used to say – the woman and I are probably shirt-tail cousins – give-or-take a few generations."

Hasna had luckily snatched Kareem from the road when a jeep-load of British soldiers had driven by. They had been traveling so fast, that only her practically wrenching Kareem's arm from his shoulder had saved him from being run over. She had hurled a few curses at the soldiers that were lost in the sound of the wheels churning up a cloud of dust. She thought that the curses had been appropriate *wishing* that God would *destroy their homes,* and the homes of the *men who had "planted" them.* She would have wished something worse, but her knowledge of curses was limited.

The hunt for rebel leaders was relentless. In addition to the British troops and Zionist gangs, forces from the Transjordan regime were also engaged in the hunt. It was thought advisable to form *peace detachments* – small mercenary bands of *local* peasants who would cooperate with the British, and who would assist in hunting down the rebels by *identifying* the rebel leaders and their followers, and *supplying* this information to the British.

Money talks sometimes more loudly than fear, Officer Webb used to say to his fellow officers. *Some men will do just about anything for money,* he had said. *But the winning combination is money and fear!*

It was about this time that Ibrahim, the young man who had been detained when Mansur and Khalil were, was re-arrested. It was thought with the -*proper encouragement* – that his services could be drafted as a member of the *peace detachment*.

The four nails that had been ripped from his fingers had not completely grown back. He wondered if they ever would. His hands still ached when he tried to make a fist. The cigarette burns on his genitals had left scars. There were permanent ink splotches under each eye. However, the invisible scars tattooed on his spirit were the worst. They had changed him. They had altered who he was. He *knew* he would do anything not to be hurt like that again.

He was dragged into the interrogation room. He even recognized one of the men – a man who had burned him with cigarettes and had made fun of his shriveled penis. He felt his back grow damp with sweat; his legs began to shake involuntarily; he thought he was going to wet himself.

They asked him questions that he couldn't answer. He couldn't answer because he couldn't understand what they were asking. It was as though his mind had put on armor. One statement finally seemed to pierce through the mental mist of his mind. "If you cooperate with us, we will give you money and release you. All you need to do is *listen* and *report*. We want you to find out who the rebel leaders are in your area and who the members of their gangs are. That's all you need to do, *habeebee. Listen* and *report.*" The interrogator paused. "However, *habeebee,* if you don't, there are ways – *unfortunate* ways – to *persuade* you."

Ibrahim didn't know what to say. His tongue seemed like it was coated with fur, or as if he had a mouth full of feathers. He tried to speak, but he couldn't.

They waited. Then they acted.

He was lifted from the chair, his fingers wrenched from the grip they had on the chair's arms. He was dragged into another room and there he was tied hand and foot to a board. A canvas bag was placed over his head and a pitcher of water was poured over the bag. He couldn't catch his breath; he thought his lungs would burst. He kept struggling and twisting his head from side to side. More water was poured over the bag.

Finally the fur around his tongue and the feathers in his mouth seemed to dissolve. He screamed that he would do anything – anything – just stop!

They stopped.

He was dragged back to a cell and kept in isolation. He fitfully slept and dreamt of Mansur, Khalil and Abu Waleed. He moaned in his sleep and wept.

Two days later he again was taken into the interrogation room. This time he listened to what they said. He said nothing; he only looked at the table and nodded his head. He was told that there would be one man who would be his *contact.* This man would meet him once a week, and if the information that was given was *good,* he would be paid. He was told to raise his eyes and *look* at his contact. He looked with empty eyes at the man who had tortured him.

Ibrahim was released.

When he was gone, the interrogators had talked among themselves.

"Do you think he can be trusted?" one asked.

"No problem. He is a broken man. He won't want to be *persuaded* again," the man who had tortured him laughed. "He's our man now."

Several days later Ibrahim went to see Abu Waleed. Abu Waleed went with him to see Mansur and Khalil. When the four of them were together, Ibrahim told what had happened to him. He told what the interrogators wanted him to do. He told about the plan he had hatched.

Mansur, Khalil, and Abu Waleed listened and grimly nodded their heads.

"We will help you," they each said in turn. "When are you to meet your contact?"

"Two weeks from Friday he is to come to the olive grove on the hillside near my village. He is to come just after dusk. I am to be waiting there."

"We will be waiting with you; waiting where he cannot see us."

"You are a brave man, Ibrahim." Mansur said.

"They think I am weak. They think they have broken me. They have made me *strong* by ripping out my fingernails; they have watered my hatred when they tied me to the board, put a sack over my head and poured water on me until I thought I would drown. I will have my *revenge!*

There was fierceness in Ibrahim's eyes.

"I will *let* them think that I am weak, and broken, and *their man*. And when the time is right..."

Chapter 28

The gears of the ancient bus groaned as the driver shifted into low to make the steep climb up the narrow, serpentine road that slithered its way along the side of the mountain. The tires slipped a bit as they sought for traction. Ibrahim looked out the side window and down into a rocky ravine with stunted trees, stone walls in disrepair, two figures winding their way up the side of the mountain. They were so far away that he could not see them distinctly. He could only tell that one was a man from his white *kuffiyeh* and trousers. The skirt of his *umbaz* was tucked into his sash. The other was a woman, *probably his wife,* Ibrahim thought. She was balancing a *plowshare* on her head.

The bus teetered on the edge; the wheels sought leverage as an armored car passed them coming from the other direction. The road was barely wide enough for two vehicles. For a moment Ibrahim thought that the bus would plunge into the valley below. He could *see* the bus plummeting into the valley, bouncing off the stone terraces, uprooting the stunted trees and mowing down the old man with the skirt of his *umbaz* tucked into his trousers and the woman balancing the plowshare on her head.

The threadbare tires hugged the road. The bus seemed to shiver in relief as it once again began the climb up the hill.

Ibrahim's mind was troubled. He absentmindedly rubbed the fingers with their half-healed nails. His breath came in pained gasps as though remembering the water-soaked canvas bag and the sensation of drowning. The rusty stains of blood – *his blood* – still dotted the skirt of his *umbaz*. His mother had not been able to wash the stains away. *The garment is too good to throw away, she had said.* The stains had faded, the material weakened where his mother had scrubbed it against her knuckles; the stains had been bleached by the sun to where they were barely visible, but for Ibrahim they were still bright red.

He knew he had been *chosen – chosen by God*. He knew that what he plotted to do had been *written;* that it was his *naseeb* – his destiny, his fate! He smiled a bit, the dark, wounded shadows under his eyes contracting the smile. A little boy in the seat right across from Ibrahim glanced at his face and quickly turned around. There was something in the man's eyes that scared him.

"I'll show them. I'll show them. I'll show them," Ibrahim muttered to himself. His lips barely moved under the beginnings of a moustache. He rubbed his injured fingers over the rusty stains on the skirt of his *umbaz*.

Mansur caressed the end of Hasna's braid that lay against his chest. He rubbed the red strands between his calloused fingers.

"I'm worried about Ibrahim," he said.

"He has been sorely hurt," Hasna said gently moving her hand through the forest of hair on Mansur's chest.

"Yes, he *has* been badly wounded," Mansur paused but continued to absently rub the end of her braid. "It is the wounds that *cannot be seen* that trouble me."

"You *will* help him? You and Khalil, and your friend, Abu Waleed?" Hasna asked.

"Of course, he is like our younger brother or *son*. He is *family*. We will do all that we can to assist him, to protect him, to see that he does not come to further harm."

For some moments Hasna did not speak. Mansur thought that she had fallen asleep and gently kissed the top of her red curls.

"Even if it means helping him *kill?*" Hasna whispered against his chest.

"Inshallah it will not come to that," Mansur whispered as he tightened his arms about her.

Routine punctuated the days that followed. There was a distinct division of tasks dictated by gender. Hasna fetched the water from the well; ground the flour on an old stone mill; baked the daily bread; washed and mended the clothes; prepared the meals; cleaned the house; gathered brush for kindling – though she did elicit the aid of Omar and Khalil in the collection of brush, and dung to dry for fuel, in the gathering of fodder for the sheep, goats, and donkey and in the milking of the goats – and, of course, caring for the children.

It seemed that no matter what the task, she *always* had a child or two in tow. Kareem still did not venture too far from the grasp of her skirt; Jameel still needed to ride on a hip or straddle her shoulder, and Imad had to be carried in his swaddled cocoon.

When there wasn't plowing to do, or stone walls to repair, or fields to be tended, or harvests to be gathered, Mansur chopped wood, repaired tools, slaughtered animals – when there were animals to be slaughtered – and did all those things that demanded he be out in public.

It was Mansur who sold the ram.

Even though he and Hasna *both knew* he should sell the *young* ram, it was the *old* ram that Mansur dragged by its ear out the gate. The ram bleated mournfully in protest. Khalil walked behind the ram switching its wooly rump. *"Yallah, Yallah,"* he said.

Mansur had not forgiven himself for slapping Hasna, though *she* had forgiven him. He had repeated arguments with himself over it. *There were times when a wife needed to be disciplined. It said so in the Quran,* he argued. *Yet, Hasna was right. The young ram was special. Abdallah had died as a result of trying to save it,* he reasoned. *But a wife should never contradict her husband in front of his children,* he told himself. *Still, he would rather have cut off his hand than to have raised it against Hasna!*

He, consequently, couldn't bring himself to sell the young ram.

When Omar brought the sheep and goats back from the hills that evening, Hasna was waiting at the door of the *qa'albayt*. She had Jameel on her hip, and of course, Kareem clutching her skirt. As the young ram leaped over the threshold stone, Hasna reached down and rubbed its wooly back. "You have been saved, my fine fellow. It should have been *you* that went to the butcher's." She spoke as though the ram could understand.

When the sheep and goats had all been driven in, and the door closed behind them, Omar asked: "*Yum'ma,* why did *Yaba* take the old ram instead of the young one?"

"Your father, even though he is sometimes gruff, has a tender heart. He couldn't bring himself to sell the young ram because it was Abdallah's lamb and because..."

"Because what, *Yum'ma?*" Omar asked.

Hasna looked thoughtfully at her son, a son who looked very much like Mansur. "Because he loves us, and he knew..." Hasna paused as she looked into the distance, "he knew how much the ram meant to me."

Ibrahim had not been able to sleep for days. At night he lay awake: plotting, planning, rehearsing, just how he would take his revenge. During the day he was restless.

He would comb the hills talking to himself, finding comfort in *hearing* the plan. He could *visualize* what he would *do* to the British soldiers who had tortured him. In his visions, *he was always brave and strong and steadfast.* In his visions, *he was never afraid; he never begged; he never cried!* In his visions, *he was a man to be feared!*

On one of his daily walks through the hills he had come upon an old, abandoned cistern. It was in the shape of a pear – deep, and dark, and dry. *It must have had a crack in it,* Ibrahim thought. *That is why it no longer holds water.*

He peered down into the cistern's cavern. It was deep – deeper than the height of two men. The pear-shape made it impossible for a man, once dumped into it, to be able to climb out. He could make out in the shadowy depths, the bones of an animal which must have fallen into the cistern.

The top of the cistern was gone. *The opening can easily be covered with brush,* he thought. *It is too remote for the shouts of a man to be heard;* he smiled to himself – a far away gleam in his eye. *It is perfect.*

As Ibrahim made his way down the side of the mountain, he said a prayer of thanks to God. He had been *shown* the way.

Chapter 29

There was a crescent moon the night of the scheduled rendezvous. The stars looked down with brilliant indulgence on the rocky hills, the stone terraces, the stunted shrubs. Mansur, Khalil, and Abu Waleed were hidden in the darkness – silent observers of the scene enacted a short distance from them.

Ibrahim waited, a barely discernible silhouette, pacing beneath a gnarled olive tree.

"There he is," whispered Abu Waleed to his two companions. "There he is," he pointed.

A figure could be seen slowly climbing up the mountain side. His curses punctuated the darkness as he stumbled over the rocks. He was *not* alone.

The man called: "Ibrahim? Ibrahim, where are you?" He then said something to his companion who turned and went back down the hill.

"Ibrahim," the man called again as he continued to stumble up the hill. "Where in bloody hell are you?"

Ibrahim did not answer.

When Ibrahim had seen the companion disappear from sight, he stepped from the screen of the olive tree.

"Over here. I'm over here," he whispered. His words were barely audible above the night sounds.

The man stepped into the light of the crescent moon. Ibrahim looked at it and remarked almost casually, "It looks like the sickle we peasants use to cut the grain. If you look closely, those stars almost look like the handle."

"Have you got any information for me?" the man asked in his fractured Arabic. There was irritation in his voice.

"Information? Was I to give you information?" Ibrahim paused. "Ah, yes, I was to find out about rebel leaders and those who follow them. I remember now. You're going to *pay* me aren't you? And...if I don't tell you...you are going to *hurt* me. Yes, it is all clear to me now."

The man could hardly control his anger. "I want *names!*" he shouted in whispers. "Names! Or so help me..." he sputtered.

Ibrahim moved close enough to him so his words could be *felt* on the man's lips.

"You think that I am weak," Ibrahim smiled. "You think that I am broken," he spat, his spittle landing on the man's lips. "You think that, *for money*, I will betray my people." Ibrahim stopped and grabbed the man's arms, pinning them to his sides.

The man struggled. He was strong, but not strong enough for the insanity that possessed Ibrahim at that moment.

"You think that I am afraid of you. What can you possibly do to me that you have not already done?" Ibrahim asked shaking the man.

Ibrahim began to push. He pushed the man toward the open mouth of the cistern.

"You're mad!" the man gasped. "Bloody hell!"

He struggled and stumbled and almost fell as Ibrahim continued to push him. He was surprised at the strength in the youth's hands.

When they had reached the gaping mouth of the cistern, Ibrahim reached down and picked up the sickle he had placed there. Before the man could utter a sound, Ibrahim sliced through his neck as though he was slicing through the stalks of wheat. He pushed and the body fell into the dark cavern of the cistern.

Mansur, Khalil, and Abu Waleed were shocked. They quietly, almost magically, appeared at Ibrahim's side.

"What have you done? He has a companion who will be looking for him!" Khalil hissed in Ibrahim's ear.

"We must cover the opening with brush," Abu Waleed said as he tossed the sickle into the dark depths and frantically started pulling brush over the cistern's mouth.

Mansur strongly gripped Ibrahim by the shoulders and looked into his empty eyes.

"I have done it...I have done it...I have proved myself a man; he will never hurt me again; he will never hurt me again," Ibrahim kept repeating as he stared into Mansur's anxious eyes.

"We must get him away from here," Abu Waleed urged. "I don't think that the other man saw that Ibrahim was here. He will think that the man stumbled in the darkness and fell into the well."

"Fell into the well and *sliced his neck with a sickle on the way down?*" Khalil silently exploded. "When the body is found, the authorities will know that it is murder. People from the village will be punished."

"Punished? Who will be punished?" Ibrahim asked. He was so intent on taking revenge, that he had forgotten that an entire village was punished if the culprit could not be found. There would be house-to-house searches; there would be mass arrests of all the village men; there would be destruction of houses. *That must not happen,* he thought to himself.

"No one must be punished for what I have done. I will wait here for the man's companion," he said sitting abruptly down on the stone wall.

He was almost *calm* as he sat on the wall beneath the sickle moon and under the silent stars.

"*This* is my *naseeb. This* is what has been written for me."

"You, my friends, must go. You must not be found here, or you too will be blamed."

A voice called from the road. The companion was coming back.

"GO!" Ibrahim insisted.

The three men hugged Ibrahim. Their eyes were wet with tears as they hurried back into the stunted trees and let the darkness veil their presence. They *knew* that he would be caught. They *knew* that it was better for one to be punished, than for an entire village to be punished. They *knew* it was wrong to commit unjustified murder, but to them *this was not murder*. They *knew* that there had been no recourse. The law would not protect them – *hadn't* protected Ibrahim. If the law did not protect a man, then he must *protect* himself. The Quran was clear about the justice of an eye-for-an-eye.

"We must wait," Mansur whispered to the others. "We must wait and pray. We must wait so he knows that he is not alone."

They watched as Ibrahim pointed to the cistern. They watched as the soldier flashed his torch down into the black depths. They watched as he bound Ibrahim's hands and pulled him down the mountainside. Ibrahim did not resist.

Ibrahim was in prison for several weeks. A Military Tribunal found him guilty of murder and sentenced him to be hanged.

The morning of the hanging was cool and crisp. As he faced east that morning and knelt in prayer, he felt an inexplicable peace. He thought of his parents, his siblings, of his friends: Mansur, Khalil, and Abu Waleed. He prayed that Allah would bless them.

Death is the destiny of all, he thought. *We live the days that are allotted to us, and then we are taken back to God. This is my naseeb – my fate. I am content.*

He put the small, white skull cap on his head and removed his sandals. He smiled as he remembered his grandmother's wish to *die with the dust still on her feet.* He would die with the dust still on his feet; that was why he had removed his sandals. He wanted to walk barefooted to the gallows. He had been told by one of the other prisoners that sometimes a man's bowels moved when he was hung. He hoped that wouldn't be true for him.

The sun had not reached its summit when the guards came for him. His hands were tied behind his back. The sash on his *umbaz* was removed. A guard held him on each side and led him out into the sun of the prison courtyard. He could see the gallows ahead of him.

The dusty stones of the courtyard felt warm to his bare feet. He kept his head high and walked unfalteringly. There was a calmness – a peace – the first real peace he had felt in a long time. The last several weeks his moustache had finally come in fuller. He could slip his tongue between his lips and touch the wiry bristles of his moustache.

He stumbled on the first step, but luckily caught himself before he fell. The two guards positioned him above the trap door. The noose was placed over his head. The knot was tightened around his throat. Ibrahim looked above the heads of the men who had come to observe. Fluffy white clouds floated in a blue sea of sky. He was going *home.*

The trapdoor opened. He dropped. Blackness enveloped him. His bowels *did* move, but he wasn't aware of it. He gently swung in the morning breeze. Side to side he swung on the rope swing.

Colin Thatcher was eighteen. This was his first tour of duty. He had looked forward to the adventure of being away from home, of being on his own. He had anticipated the thrill of traveling, of being in a foreign land. He had been raised Free Methodist and he felt it was a blessing from God that he was stationed in the Holy Land. His comrades had kidded him about being *religious.* It was alright, *they are basically good blokes,* he thought.

As he watched the criminal swing, he shuddered. He had held one of his arms as he was marched to the gallows. The prisoner was just a kid. *He's younger than me,* Colin thought. Oh, he knew what the boy had done, but he had also noticed the bloke's fingers where the nails had been pulled off. He had been assigned to watch him when he took his last shower. He hadn't wanted to look, but he had seen the scars on his genitals. *The kid had taken a proper beating,* he thought to himself.

As he watched him swing, he tried to suppress the thought that he could *understand* why he had done what he had done. He tried to suppress the thought, that had he been in the kid's place he may have *done the same thing.*

Ibrahim was left to swing for a while. He was eventually taken down and plopped into a wooden box. The box was delivered to his parents.

He was hanged three days before his seventeenth birthday.

Mansur and Khalil had heard from Abu Waleed about the funeral. They, with Hasna, made the journey by bus to Ibrahim's village.

Hasna sat with the women from the village. She joined with them in singing the wedding songs that would have been sung for a *bridegroom.* The songs that were traditionally sung at a wedding were sung at a funeral when the man was young and had not yet been married. The women wept as they sang. Ibrahim had been laid out on a pallet in his father's one-room house. Wrapped in a blanket, he was completely covered except for his face. The dark splotches under his eyes looked like they had been outlined in *kohl.* He was handsome.

When the men came to take the body, the women stood up and began to trill: hands raised against the side of their mouths as their tongues moved rapidly side-to-side. *The bridegroom was leaving the house.* They trilled, the tears flowing unhindered down their cheeks.

Mansur, Khalil and Abu Waleed were among the men who took turns carrying the coffin to the graveyard. They raised the box high off their shoulders and chanted: *Allahu Akbar! Allahu Akbar!* (God is Greater).

Ibrahim was taken from the wooden box. His older brothers stood in the grave ready to receive the shrouded body of their younger brother. They lovingly positioned him.

The men waited while the wooden planks were placed over the body. They waited while the dirt and stones were placed upon the planks. They waited until the grave was closed.

Mansur, Khalil, and Abu Waleed shook hands with the members of Ibrahim's family and offered words of condolence. They kissed his aged father on both cheeks. Mansur hugged him and whispered brokenly into his ear, "You can be proud of your son. He was a brave man. He has brought honor to your house. He was a martyr."

Chapter 30

A small gray mouse peered at Hasna as she made bread. He peeked from behind an earthenware jar of olives. Hasna *hated* mice and could understand her mother's tolerance of the black snake that used to live in the *qa'albayt*. She had been happy, shortly after marrying Mansur, to discover that a black snake also inhabited their *qa'albayt. Black snakes may suck eggs if they have the chance, but they also eat mice,* she thought in defense of the slithery creatures. She never allowed the children to kill a black snake.

The year she had married Mansur the wheat crop had almost been completely destroyed by battalions of *field mice.* They swarmed over the fields in hoards – a gray blanket of pulsing vermin – plundering the young, green shoots. Their whiskered mouths were tiny, their nibbles small, but there were *hundreds.*

Hasna was also not too fond of starlings. A massive migration of starlings, a year or so – before or after the depredations of the field mice, she couldn't quite remember if it had been *before* or *after* –had practically robbed the fields of all the newly planted seed. She could remember rushing out to the field with her mother screeching at the birds, waving her head shawl, trying to get the birds to *fly away.*

Perhaps worse than the foraging field mice and starving starlings were the plagues of locusts. For four consecutive years voracious locusts had blackened the sky and descended on the fields. They had gone out to the fields with metal pots and wooden spoons and made noise to get the locusts to *move. Oh, they had moved alright,* she thought, *after there was nothing left to eat.*

She sometimes, in her frustrated ignorance, wondered if God (May He forgive her) *really* knew what He was about. Sometimes the rains were early; sometimes the rains were late; sometimes there were long periods of drought; sometimes there were floods and so much rain that the newly planted seed was washed from the fields. Sometimes there was seed to plant; sometimes there was no seed to plant.

All of these natural disasters had contributed to the impoverishment of the peasant. When the crops *had* survived and the yield had been relatively good, there were no *markets* for the produce. On those occasions when there *had been* markets, the price was so low that the farmers barely covered the cost of the seed they had bought and they still had to pay the moneylenders, the tax collectors, and in some cases the landowners. The farmer reaped little, *if anything,* from his labor. It was easy to become depressed and to think *why bother.*

Adding to the rural mosaic was the political unrest created by the British Mandate, the Zionist encroachment, a weak Arab political system, and the rebel bands.

The bruised rural economy had caused the farmers to be angry with the British who occupied them and put them down, fearful of their harsh punishments. They were frustrated with the influx of Jewish settlers, who were helping the British and at the same time helping their selves to the land. It was natural that they would join the rebel bands. It seemed right to shoot at British soldiers from behind a stone wall, or from around a gnarled olive tree; it seemed *justified* to burn the fields of Jewish settlers, to tear down their fences; to shoot into their settlements. It was natural to turn a deaf ear to the instructions of some village *mukhtars* who seemed to be the mouthpieces for the Mandate government, or for corrupt Arab leaders, unscrupulous moneylenders or absent landlords. There were so many reasons to want to *lash out*. For some, the rebel bands were an answer, however inadequate, ill-equipped, unorganized, or doomed to fail.

Both Mansur and Khalil had been sorely tempted, especially after the hanging of Ibrahim, to join a rebel band. They also, like so many others, were fearful, frustrated, and *angry!* They desperately wanted to *do something*. The words of the bearded stranger had planted the seeds of rebellion in their spirits. The month in prison had added fertilizer to those seeds. The death of the youth, Ibrahim, had watered their determination. The current instability and insecurity of their lives inflamed their resolve.

They weren't afraid of a fight. They didn't fear death – in fact at times they thought it would be a *welcome relief!* Did not the Quran promise an eternity of crystal clear waters, couches upon which to repose, and lovely maidens with doe-like eyes? Did not the Imams preach that this life was but *amusement and a testing?* Were they not taught that the *real home* was the home in heaven? No, *death* was not something to fear, especially when one was dying in a righteous cause and one could anticipate a heavenly reward.

They *were*, however, concerned about their families. If they had been single, there would have been no doubt at all, no hesitation. But the fact that they were both married and had small children whose survival depended on them gave them pause.

It was 1938 and the strike and rebellion had been going on for two years. There had been: house searches, night raids, curfews, arrests, imprisonments, canings, floggings, deportations, hangings, torture. There were more than *sufficient reasons* to join a band.

In 1938 Mansur was twenty-six, Hasna was twenty-one and they had *five* sons and another baby was on the way. *If something happens to me, what will become of Hasna and our children?* Mansur thought. He would argue with himself that *God would provide for them.* Hasna would, in her gentle way, suggest that God *was* providing for them – He had provided them with Mansur!

It wasn't always *easy* for Hasna to make *gentle suggestions.* She had a willful obstinacy that accompanied her red hair. She *knew*, at least most of the time, that she was *right* and that she saw things more clearly than Mansur did. She also *knew* that she needed to bite her tongue when arguing; that she had to *listen* and then *suggest* rather than *state.*

Mansur was not really conscious of how dependent he had become on Hasna's *suggestions.* He only knew that after discussing things with her; after voicing his thoughts; after listening to her quiet, whispered suggestions – that his thoughts *did* become clearer.

Hasna was no longer the shy, thirteen-year-old he had married. She wore a worn, threadbare *thob* with just a hint of frayed embroidery on the chest panel and skirt. The bottoms of her feet were heavily calloused from going barefooted most of the time. Her hands were rough and red from all the work she did, and in the winter months were blistered with chilblains. Her sons were not aware that she was raising them with an iron hand. She brooked no objections, but she had a way about her of smiling, and laughing, and hugging, and teasing that made them idolize her. They did her bidding as faithful servants would. She made them feel like little *princes* and they consequently thought she was the beautiful red-haired, blue-eyed, freckled *queen* of the tales she sometimes spun.

In this year of 1938 her little, barefoot *princes* in their raggedy *dash-a-deesh* were *almost* eight, six, five, three, and one. The new baby – whom she hoped was a *princess* – swam and cavorted in the safety of the womb.

Hasna was carrying this baby higher than she had the others; thus she was convinced that this baby would be a girl. The aged midwife, Im Hussein, also thought she was carrying a girl this time.

At night when Mansur would lay his hand on her belly to feel the baby *swim,* Hasna would place her hand on top of his and smile. "That is your daughter," she would say. He would smile tenderly at her and whisper, "It seems she is going to be as lively as her mother; this little *Hourieh* of ours."

Hasna went into labor in late December. It was cold. It was rainy. She had chilblains on her fingers and on her toes. It didn't seem as though she was ever warm. The children wore layers of clothes – all the clothes they owned in fact. During the day there was no heat in the house. At night, for an hour or so, Mansur would light a brazier around which they would sit before lying down on their pallets and snuggling beneath the thick cotton comforters. The comforters were so heavy that the children could barely *move* under them.

Hasna went into labor in the morning. Unlike the labor when Imad had been born, this labor seemed to go on and on and on. *I know it's a girl,* Hasna thought. *This labor is different.* Her labor continued, off and on, all day. Mansur kept asking if he should send for the midwife, and Hasna kept saying, "Not yet."

Finally after about ten hours of labor she told Mansur to take the children to Khalil's house for Zareefeh to watch, and to go and call the midwife.

Sitteh Im Hussein arrived with two older neighbor women who were past menopause and who assisted her in deliveries. They brought with them the birthing stone, a straw basket of dirt, and a bundle of rags.

She examined Hasna and could see that she had already dilated. Im Hussein could insert four fingers into her womb and touch the head.

"Good, the little one has dropped and is already presenting himself in the birth canal."

"You mean *herself*," Hasna muttered around a strong contraction.

Im Hussein smiled, "*Her*self," she corrected.

Hasna hovered over the birthing stone, her *thob* bunched around her waist. The two older women turned their backs toward Hasna and linked arms. Hasna braced herself against their backs, pressed her hands against her extended belly, and grunted as she pushed. The baby moved a little.

Im Hussein again examined her. "Push again."

Hasna's freckled face grew red as she strained. Her face was damp with sweat. There were rivulets of sweat running down her quivering legs. Again she pushed.

"Stop. Breathe. Rest." Im Hussein instructed. Hasna panted and blew air from her mouth.

"Now! One strong push!"

Hasna gave a low moan as the baby finally tore itself free from the birth canal.

Im Hussein caught the wet, red infant. Grasping the two legs in one hand, she turned the baby upside down and gave him a sound swat on the buttocks.

The two older women had turned around and were supporting Hasna. They lowered her to the pallet on the floor. Im Hussein placed the squalling infant on Hasna's chest. She did not cut the cord until the afterbirth had descended and been pushed out.

The women quickly swept up the bloody earth, moved the birthing stone, and placed the afterbirth in the basket. They then washed the blood off Hasna's legs and cleaned her up.

Im Hussein had cut the cord. The baby had dozed off, cradled against Hasna's chest, held in her arms. Hasna was exhausted as she smiled at this new addition. She counted the fingers and toes with rough, chilblained fingers.

"We were both wrong," Im Hussein joked with her. "You have another *son.*"

"Yes, but this son is unlike his brothers. This son has *red* hair."

Chapter 31

Stone steps climbed up the side of the house to the domed roof. They had been constructed so the workers could reach the roof and make the dome. They had also been built with the belief that one day a second story would be added for a married son. At the moment, it looked as though they were the beginning of stairs to the stars.

Hasna faithfully kept the steps swept. She liked to sit on the roof, her back resting against the dome, her feet practically dangling over the edge, and gaze at the beauty of the rugged hills; the morning sky painted in brilliant reds and yellows; the evening sky just before the sun went down and dropped its dusky veil. She liked the view of Jerusalem in the distance – lights twinkling like the stars above.

There were times when she took five little boys up to the roof. They daringly wanted to dangle their legs over the edge, but Hasna never let them. They would sit around her, like chicks around a mother hen, and she would tell stories.

Sometimes they were stories about the adventures of the mischievous *Juha*.

"One day a neighbor came to Juha and wanted to borrow his donkey," Hasan said. *"And Juha didn't want to lend*

his donkey to this neighbor so he said, 'Alas and a day, my donkey took sick and died.'"

Hasna paused to look into the intent faces of her sons.

"Just then, Juha's donkey brayed! The neighbor knew that Juha was stretching the truth," Hasna said.

"'But, Juha, I just heard your donkey bray!' the neighbor said. Juha looked at the man and said, 'Who are you going to believe, me or my donkey?'"

"Tell us another story, *Yum'ma,"* Kareem begged. Hasna put her arms around the two littlest ones and told the story of Juha and the brass pot.

"Once Juha was having a dinner for his family and he needed a big cauldron in which to cook the stew. Juha didn't have a large enough pot so he went to his neighbor to borrow one. The neighbor reluctantly lent a cauldron to Juha. The next day Juha promptly returned the cauldron. When the neighbor looked inside she saw a small brass cooking pot. She was delighted. She asked Juha about the pot. He replied, 'When your cauldron was visiting it gave birth to this little brass pot.'"

"How can a pot give birth?" Khalil asked.

"You'll see," Hasna answered.

"A week later Juha had another dinner and once again went to borrow the cauldron from his neighbor. This time the neighbor was more than willing to lend it to Juha thinking she would get another small brass pot. A week passed; two weeks passed; three weeks passed and still Juha did not return the cauldron. Finally the neighbor

woman went to Juha to demand that he return her cauldron. When she asked Juha about it, he sadly shook his head and sighed. 'Alas and a day, when your cauldron came to visit, it died.' 'How can a cauldron die?' the woman asked angrily. The mischievous Juha replied, 'If a cauldron can give birth, it can surely die.'"

Sometimes if it was dusk and Hasna and the children were on the roof listening to stories, Mansur would climb the stairs so he could also listen to Hasna's tales. He would joke with Hasna that he had come up to carry the two littlest ones down, but she knew that he liked her stories as much as the children did.

Sometimes Mansur would be startled by the realization that in spite of all the seeming disconnectedness of their lives, the one real connection – the one thread that seemed to run through all the events of their lives – was *Hasna*. He would thank God that he had had that dream of the girl he should marry having red-hair, blue eyes and freckles!

In late September of 1938 Abu Waleed came to visit. They had not seen him since Ibrahim's funeral. It was Abu Waleed who told them the story of the massacre at Al-Bassa – a small village in the north of the country, very close to the Lebanese border.

They were sitting outside in the courtyard, Mansur and Hasna, Khalil and Zareefeh, Abu and Im Mansur, and Hasna's two teen-age brothers, Saif and Ali. It was cool enough that Mansur had lit the brass *kanoon* and they had pulled their low, caned-bottomed stools around it.

"Im Waleed's sister is married to a man from al-Bassa – a village in the north. It is from her that I heard what happened," Abu Waleed began warming his hands against the dancing flames of the *kanoon.*

"Four British soldiers were killed just outside the village. It seems that the jeep they were in ran over a mine that had been planted in the road." Abu Waleed paused and stroked his shaggy moustache.

"The village *mukhtars* had been warned that if there were any *incidents* the nearest village would be punished. Of course, the death of four British soldiers was not just *any incident!* The British commander in the area was enraged. And naturally so," Abu Waleed added. "He felt that *immediate* reprisal was needed."

"He ordered his men into the village. The inhabitants were routed out of their houses and taken to the outskirts of the village where they were surrounded by armed soldiers. Some of the soldiers then went into each house and lit the braziers and spilled the hot coals onto the straw mats and pallets. They splashed petrol onto the floors and wall – they set fire to the village, destroying most of the houses."

His audience listened, too stunned to comment.

"While the village was burning, the commander ordered that the men line up and he randomly picked fifty. Among them was Im Waleed's sister's husband," Abu Waleed continued.

"There was a bus parked at the outskirts of the village. The British commander then ordered twenty of the men onto the bus. Some tried to run away and were shot. When twenty were on the bus, the driver was told to get behind the wheel." Again Abu Waleed paused.

"Two soldiers were ordered to place a mine in the center of the road some distance from the village, but within sight of the assembled villagers." He stopped as though looking for the right words.

"The bus driver was ordered to drive the bus over the mine."

The "*No!*" of disbelief came in unison from the listeners.

"He did. The bus blew up sending fragments of metal and pieces of bodies onto the road and into the brush that lined it. My brother-in-law was one of the men on the bus."

"What happened then," Mansur asked in a stunned voice.

"Some men from the village were ordered to dig a large pit. Other men were ordered to pick-up the pieces of their neighbors, brothers, fathers, sons, and to throw them into the pit. The pit was then covered...a mass grave."

"It is no wonder that we hate them so," Khalil uttered into the stillness.

Saif and Ali had listened to the story in shocked silence.

It was the next morning that Awad brought the news that Saif and Ali had disappeared. They had left without a word, but their father's old hunting rifle and that of Awad's were gone from where they had been hidden beneath the straw.

About two months later, in the middle of the night, there was a muffled knock on the wooden door. Hasna heard it first. She gently shook Mansur awake. "I think there is someone at the door," she whispered.

Mansur blinked the sleep from his eyes. He, too, had heard the muffled knock. "Stay here," he whispered to Hasna.

Going to the door he asked, "Who's there?"

"It is us, Saif and Ali."

Mansur immediately raised the iron hook and opened the wooden door.

Before him stood his two brothers-in-law, bearded and scraggly looking; each was gripping a rifle in his hand. "Come in. Come in," he whispered hugging them both and kissing them on both cheeks.

As soon as Hasna had seen who was at the door, she had lit a kerosene lamp and stood at Mansur's side. She, too, hugged and kissed her brothers.

"Where have you been? You must be hungry?" she said not waiting for their reply.

She pulled out bread and cheese; she got out dried figs and raisins; she put out dishes of olive oil and thyme; she pumped the primus and put on a kettle of water to boil for tea.

Mansur had pulled their pallet against a far wall – away from the sleeping children. The three men sat on the pallet and leaned their backs against the stone wall.

Hasna brought the tray of food and placed the tray on the stone floor before them. Positioning herself next to Mansur she listened to the tale her brothers had to tell.

"The evening we left – that evening after hearing Abu Waleed's story – we dug out from beneath the straw our father's old hunting rifle, and that of Awad. We could only find a dozen bullets," Saif said.

"We walked all night. We thought we knew" Ali added, "where a rebel band was camped. Luckily, we were found by Hosni."

"Who is Hosni?" Hasna asked.

"It is better if you don't know his full name or where he is from," Saif replied.

"Hosni was a member of the rebel band we were seeking. He took us to them. It was Hosni who took us under his wing. He taught us how to fire our guns. Hosni taught us how to be guerrillas."

Hasna poured more tea into their glasses.

"We need some help. That's why we have come to you," Saif said looking at his sister and brother-in-law. "We need food. And," he paused, "we need money to buy bullets."

"We know you don't have much money," Ali added. "But whatever you could spare would help."

Mansur looked at Hasna and nodded. She went to the bridal chest that had once belonged to Abdallah's mother, and taking the key from the embroidered box in which she kept threads and scissors, she unlocked the chest. From the depths she drew a small linen sack. Taking the sack she placed it in Saif's hand.

"This is all we have, but you are welcome to it." Saif smiled gratefully at his sister as he tucked the small sack into his sash. "Thank you, this will help more than you know."

Hasna then busied herself in gathering food for her brothers to carry back with them. She spread a *kuffiyeh* on the floor and began piling into it: dried figs, containers of olives, goat cheese, raisins; all the bread she had baked that day; she tied into a clean rag loose black tea; she added bundles of dried herbs – anything she could think of she put on the pile. Finally she tied the ends of the *kuffiyeh* together and gave the bundle to Ali.

"We must be going; it will soon be daylight. Thank you," Saif said hugging his sister.

Hasna placed her hand above his heart, "Remember I am always here," she whispered to him.

"I know," he whispered with tears in his eyes. For a moment he was the little boy whom Hasna remembered, not this bearded youth.

"Thank you," Ali said also hugging her. She also placed her hand on his heart. "I am *always* here," she whispered trying to keep the tears from her voice.

"Take care," Mansur whispered hugging them in his strong arms. "We are so proud of you."

"*Allah ma'kum,*" Hasna said hugging them once more before they slipped into the night. "God be with you."

It was almost dawn; the morning call to prayer would soon echo over the hills; there was no point in going back to bed. They wouldn't have been able to sleep anyway.

Mansur and Hasna sat on the pallet on the floor, sipping a second glass of hot tea.

"I wonder if I will ever see them again," Hasna said looking at Mansur. There were tears in her eyes.

Chapter 32

Hasna had handed over the linen-bag of money without hesitation or discussion. Mansur knew that she would. She had looked at him before going to the bridal chest and getting the money. She had seen in his eyes that that was what *he wished* as well. He was sometimes astonished as to how often she seemed to *know exactly what he was thinking.*

He couldn't join a rebel band himself, but *at least* he could supply some money to buy some bullets. *Ibrahim had been tortured and hanged; he and Khalil, like so many others, had been imprisoned; then there was the story of the village al-Bassa and the men in the bus; guerilla fighting was the only method of fighting left open to them.* These were the thoughts that tumbled through Mansur's mind.

He was not surprised that Hasna felt as he felt. She *loved* her brothers, Saif and Ali – though not much older than they, she has helped raise them. Yet, she was proud to see them guerillas, even though it hurt her heart. She didn't question their actions; she didn't try to *talk them out* of their resolve; Mansur could *picture* her taking up a rifle herself and fighting the enemy. He could *see* the red braids framing a determined face; he could visualize those blue eyes squinting as she sighted the target and fired. *She is a gentle and loving woman,* Mansur thought. *She argued for the life of Abdallah's ram. She seems to have a soothing effect on all those around her, yet, she could kill if those around her were threatened. Yes, she supports the guerillas.* Mansur smiled at the thought of *what a warrior Hasna would be!*

Saif and Ali trudged over the rocky hillside; their rifles slung on leather straps across their backs; the tails of their *umbazes* tucked into their sashes so their trousered legs could move more rapidly. Small bits of pebble slipped into their sandals and had to be kicked out. They plodded on beneath the crescent moon and the far-flung stars. The linen pouch of money was securely anchored in Saif's sash; Ali carried the large bundle of food wrapped in the worn *kuffiyeh.*

They hadn't doubted for a moment that Mansur and Hasna would give them whatever money they had. They hadn't questioned that they could rely on them to do whatever was possible for them to do. They hadn't even *thought* of going to their brother, Awad. They had never felt close to him. He had ignored them as children and seemed to only tolerate them as youth. It was Hasna and Mansur to whom they were drawn.

They reached the rebel camp just before dawn. The campfire was only glowing embers. Some members of the band were still dozing next to the fire, wrapped up in old blankets, their rifles cradled in their sleeping arms. A sentry challenged them as they approached.

They could hear the cocking of his rifle as he whispered, "Who goes there?" They could hear the easing of the rifle's hammer as they identified themselves.

Hosni was already awake. He hugged them, patting their backs. "I'm glad you are back. Were you able to get any food, any money for ammunition?"

Saif retrieved the small linen-bag of money from his sash. "This was all we could get. It is from my sister and her husband."

Hosni weighed the small sack of money in his hand. It wasn't much, but he realized that the farmers didn't have much. As he stuffed it in his own sash he grimly smiled. "This will buy us enough bullets for a while. But we must make every bullet count."

Ali untied the bundle of food and spread it on the ground. The other members of the band began to awaken and gathered around the spread *kuffiyeh*. The water in a large kettle, blackened from the open fire, was boiling. Ali dumped in some of the loose tea that Hasna had sent. The food wasn't much, but it was enough for the men to have a good breakfast.

Every day a different man would go to a village and forage for food. The villagers, for the most part, were generous in sharing whatever they had. The village women had spread the word among themselves to prepare extra food for the rebels. It was *their* way of supporting the rebellion.

For target practice, bullets were sparingly used as bullets were too precious to waste. Sometimes the rebels burned the crops of settlers. Sometimes they tore down some of the fencing which surrounded settlements; sometimes pieces of poisoned meat were thrown at the settler's dogs. Sometimes the fighters lay in wait beneath the trees for a military jeep to pass and then opened fire. The flash of a gun going off was a spark of light in the velvet dark.

Saif and Ali would lie on their bellies, their chins almost resting in the dirt, and patiently wait for a patrol vehicle. When a truck or jeep would pass, they would take careful aim – not wanting to waste a precious bullet – and fire. Sometimes the bullet whizzed through the nighttime air, and made no contact. On other occasions the bullet found its target and there would be a groan, a body would slump over, there would be the shout in English: *I've been hit! The bloody bastards!*

Saif and Ali knew very little English, but did learn what: *hit* and *bloody bastards* meant. When they heard those words, they would wipe the sweat and dirt from their faces and grin.

The fire was *always* returned. The soldiers in the truck or jeep would pile out of the vehicle and begin firing into the trees. Sometimes the bullets from their rifles kicked up dust, dirt and splinters of rock into their faces. Sometimes they could *feel* the breeze made by the bullet as it whizzed over their heads. It was a deadly game, but a game that caused the butterflies in their stomachs to dance!

Their excursions into confrontations with the enemy were always done under the veil of night. They were not a large enough band – a strong enough band – to fight in the daylight. They were outnumbered, out-equipped, out-trained. They *weren't* professional soldiers. They were peasant farmers. They had to make use of what they *did* have: the element of surprise; the knowledge of the terrain; an anger and determination that enflamed their souls; a *willingness* to die for a just cause.

It surprisingly happened at *dawn* one morning. The shout of the sentry and a volley of rifle shots awakened them. They sprang from sleep, a bit disoriented at first, they found themselves surrounded! They returned fire as they ran up the hill; dodging the bullets that whirred above their heads, stumbling on the rocks as they bounded up the hill, seeking refuge in a cave that loomed ahead.

Saif kept urging Ali on. "Run! I've got you covered!" he screamed as he turned and fired in the direction of the advancing British soldiers.

Other men from the band were weaving back and forth as they ran over the rocky terrain and bee-lined for the entrance to the cave. A few were hit, and stumbling, flung their rifles out in front of them as they fell and slid down the mountainside.

Saif and Ali managed to reach the mouth of the cave and dive into the entrance. Hosni was already there, as was Malik, Badi', Osama and Wail.

"We are only seven – are there no more?! Are there no more?!" Hosni frantically questioned.

They took their positions at the mouth of the cave; raising their heads only to take aim and fire, then quickly ducking. Sweat stung their eyes and blurred their vision.

"How many bullets do you have?" Hosni asked.

The men counted the bullets. "I have three," said one. "I have five," said another. "Five for me as well," said a third.

They each knew that they couldn't stand off the assault. They weren't a large enough band to engage in a direct attack and have any hope of winning. They knew they couldn't just hide in the cave. They didn't want to be shot like a fox in its den.

Hosni said grimly, "We are going to die. We will die charging. We will die like *men,* not wounded dogs cowering in a hole."

He stood up and cocked his rifle, first slipping a bullet into the chamber. The others also stood up, rifles cocked. They looked grimly at each other. There was visible determination as they crawled out of the cave and charged down the mountain side. They screamed: "*Allahu Akbar! Allahu Akbar!*"

They had barely taken a few steps before their bodies were pummeled with bullets. Saif fell; his father's old hunting rifle slipping from his grasp and sliding unhindered down the side of the mountain. Its descent was finally stopped by a bit of brush. For an instant it flashed through his mind the times he had gathered brush with Hasna.

Ali saw Saif fall and had reached him just as a bullet slammed into his chest and propelled him backwards. He turned over onto his knees, though mortally wounded, he crawled over to Saif. He was able to extend his hand and grasp the lifeless hand of his brother before he too slipped into paradise.

The British soldiers gathered up the bodies of the rebel *bandits.* There were no identification papers on any of the bodies. The soldiers didn't know to which village, let alone to which families, the men belonged. They would be loaded in the back of a truck and driven through several villages as a *warning.* The bodies would then be buried in a common, unmarked grave.

Hasna had been returning from a neighbor's when the British convoy drove through the village. A loudspeaker on the truck was blaring out that a rebel band had been killed- that this is what would happen to all those who resisted.

She stood at the side of the road. All of her six children were with her. The truck drove slowly through the village so the villagers could see the pile of dead bodies.

Omar gasped as he grabbed his mother's arm. "*Yum'ma,* that's *Khali* Saif and *Khali* Ali!"

Tears streamed down her cheeks as she raised her hand to her mouth and began to trill. Other women in the street also raised their hands to their mouths and trilled. The men in the street raised their fists in the air and shouted, *"Allahu Akbar! Allahu Akbar!"*

Hasna passed the baby to Omar and taking off her worn, threadbare head shawl began to *dance* waving her shawl in the air as she trilled; her red hair bright in the afternoon sun. Zareefeh came out of the courtyard and she too began to dance. Other women in the street danced and trilled as the convoy passed.

"You'd think it was a bloody wedding," Walter Webb said as he spat tobacco juice over the side of the truck. He didn't understand the outburst of the dancing women. He thought they would be cowed – *silent at least.*

Colin Thatcher watched the dancing women; he was not deaf to their trilling; he turned away and blinked his eyes quickly, hoping his comrades had not seen the brightness of unshed tears in his eyes. He understood with a knowledge that was almost too much to bear.

Chapter 33

There were days – months after their deaths – that Hasna would pause in her work thinking she had *heard* the laughter of Saif and Ali. She would look up from whatever she was doing, and for an instant, *see* them as little boys sitting on the stone steps in her father's house, counting the sheep and goats as they leaped over the low, stone threshold into the *qa'albayt*. She would *feel* the familiar tug on her skirt and for a moment look down thinking it was the toddler, Abdallah.

There were times, in the midst of her work, when Hasna would be engulfed with a great feeling of sadness. She would remember Abdallah, Saif, and Ali – her nephew, her brothers, *her boys*. Mansur, who went to the mosque each Friday and listened to the sermon of the Imam, would tell her what he had said about heaven, and paradise, and how the children were all *in a better place*. She *wanted* to believe it was true, and part of her *did* believe it – *had to believe it!*

The Imam had said that the men who had died in the struggles against the Mandate and the Zionist encroachment went straight to heaven. The Imam had spoken of *everlasting waters, fruit of every kind, of couches of green-silk brocade on which to lie*. The Imam had spoken of eternal *peace*.

Abdallah, Saif, and Ali continued to live in her heart and mind. She often talked about them to the children and kept them *alive* for them. Evenings when they would sit on the stone stairs that climbed to the stars, she would often tell stories of when Saif and Ali and Abdallah were young. She would joke with Kareem of how he was so much like Abdallah when Abdallah was his age.

"*Yum'ma,* just like when you were little and would follow me around holding onto my skirt, Abdallah would do just the same. Before we were married, your Sitteh Im Mansur came to call. I was only thirteen-and-a-half and had come out to serve tea to your grandmothers. Abdallah was holding fast to my skirt. Your Sitteh saw how attached Abdallah was to me and me to Abdallah, that she convinced your father and your grandfather *Abu Mansur* to allow Abdallah to come and live with us. Your father would joke with me as how he had acquired a thirteen-year-old bride who already had a two-year-old son!

I can still see your father taking his little brothers-in-law, Saif and Ali, on his knee and telling them that they must come to visit every day," Hasna told the listening children.

Of course, you remember the times Saif and Ali went with us to gather brush for kindling; how they would let you two, Omar and Khalil, ride on the donkey. You were perched high on the mound of brush and Saif and Ali would rest their hands on your legs to be sure you didn't fall."

"They loved us a lot, didn't they, *Yum'ma?*" stated Omar.

"They *still* love you, *Yum'ma,*" Hasna replied. "They are sitting in heaven now – probably high among those stars – looking down on you."

The children looked into the nighttime sky. They looked at the faraway stars and *believed* that what their mother told them was true. They could *almost see* Abdallah, and Saif and Ali sitting among those stars, looking down at them and smiling.

By 1939 the rebellion began to wane. It had amazingly lasted three years; longer than the 20,000 British forces had expected; longer than the 15,000 Zionist Haganah fighting men had anticipated; longer than the disorganized, ill-trained, and - for the most-part – leaderless peasant bands had thought. But people were *weary* of the struggle.

Most of the rebel leaders had been killed; the rebels who had followed them had been either: killed, imprisoned, or fled. They hadn't been able to stand against a superior British force and the armed, organized Zionist auxiliary force the British supported. Most of the weapons in possession of the farmers had been confiscated. It was illegal for Palestinian peasants to have weapons; this policy of the Mandate, however, did not apply to Jewish settlers – *they could be armed.* Many Palestinian homes had been destroyed; thousands of Palestinian men had been imprisoned; hundreds had been wounded; hundreds had been killed. The Palestinian peasant economy was wrecked. *People were just plain tired.*

There were still, occasional, sporadic, isolated *incidents*, but *nothing* that compared to those three years of strike and rebellion. Things began to return to what went for *normalcy* among the farmers. Fields were plowed; seeds were planted; the rains came; and there were harvests.

In the spring of 1940, Mansur and Khalil arranged an outing for their families to the Dead Sea. Hasna, and of course the children, had never been to the Dead Sea. The bus trip to Jericho took a little over an hour – perhaps an hour and a half, or two hours – depending on how many times the old, rickety bus had to stop.

Hasna and Zareefeh had packed baskets of food for a picnic. They had brought blankets to spread on the sand. They had even brought a *kanoon* and skewers so they could roast the meat; *kiftah* and *kabab* over an open fire. It was a glorious day – one which they would never forget.

"Can we go in the sea, *Yum'ma?*" the children seemed to ask all at once.

"Yes," she smiled into their expectant face, "take off your *dash-a-deesh* and swim in your cotton underwear. Be sure to watch out for Imad and hold onto his hand. And don't get water in your eyes – it is salty and will sting," she shouted after them as they ran through the warm sand toward the sea.

The boys with their male cousins frolicked in the water. None of them knew how to swim, which was fine since the salty water buoyed them up. They could just lay back and were held up in the arms of the salty sea. They laughed and shouted. They splashed each other – eyes stinging from the salt.

Hasna hoisted the skirt of her *thob* up – just a bit – so she could walk barefoot along the edge of the water. She held the hands of the baby, Issa, his red curls bright in the Jericho sun, so he could also *play* in the water like his brothers. She removed his *dish-dash* and swaddling so he could sit naked in the wet sand and joyfully splash at the gentle waves that washed over his legs. He would look up at his mother with an impish grin; complete joy on his face.

Hasna looked over the sea's expanse and could see the mountains of Transjordan in the hazy distance. For the moment, the warmth of the sand; the heat of the sun; and the utter peacefulness of the day, made her forget. It was soothing balm to her spirit.

When their lunch was ready, Mansur and Khalil called to the children to come eat. There was a hand- pump on the beach where the children could wash the salt off their bodies. They screamed in delight as Mansur and Khalil poured water over their heads and rubbed the salt off their bodies with rough, calloused hands.

The picnic was perfect – at least in the eyes of the children and their parents. About four in the afternoon the bus returned. They gathered up the things they had brought and piled back in the bus. The bus would take them to Jerusalem where they would board another for their village.

By the time they got back home, they were happily exhausted. Hasna carried a sleeping Issa. Mansur carried a sleeping three-year-old, Imad. Omar and eight-year-old, Khalil, dragged a tired Kareem and Jameel. It has been such a *wonderful* break in the routine.

That night the children slept *bedun hez* (without needing to be rocked) Hasna had said to Mansur. Their curly heads had no sooner hit the pillows and they were asleep. Baby Issa slept with Omar; Imad with Khalil, and Kareem and Jameel shared a pallet. For the first time in many years, the metal cradle that usually sat by Hasna's side of the pallet she and Mansur shared was empty.

Hasna had left the shutters open on one window. "I want to see the stars," she said.

"How can you see the stars, *habeeptee? Y*our eyes will be closed," Mansur had lovingly joked with her.

"I can *see* them with my eyes closed," Hasna answered illogically.

"*See* them with your eyes closed?" Mansur chuckled as he put his arm around Hasna and she laid her head in its usual place on his chest.

"Thank you, *habeebee;* it was a perfect day," Hasna whispered, her breath gently moving the curly hairs beneath her lips. "The boys will remember this day forever."

"We will surely go again one day," Mansur murmured as his eyes began to close.

"Inshallah (God willing)" Hasna said as she too fell asleep.

Hundreds of miles away the stars had not yet come out. Colin Thatcher had finished his tour of duty in the Holy Land. Once more he was back in England. There was little mention of Palestine in the English press. The papers were full of the situation in Europe: Hitler had invaded Austria, Czechoslovakia and Poland. Italy had invaded Albania. The Jews in Germany and those in the countries invaded by the Nazis had been required to wear a yellow star sewn to their clothes.

Colin Thatcher thought about the growing number of Zionist settlements in Palestine. He had been told by a Jewish comrade, who had served with him in the British Mandate army, that there had been *50* new settlements during the 1936-1939 Arab rebellion. He knew that some European Jews would see immigration to Palestine as an escape from the persecution they were suffering in Europe. Part of him – the religious part of him – thought that this was a *right* way of thinking. *Did not the Bible say that Israel was the God-given homeland for the Jews?* Part of him knew that for that to happen, the Palestinians would have to be *pushed out.*

He couldn't seem to get out of his mind the vision of the young Palestinian man who had been hanged. He couldn't seem to forget the picture of that truckload of dead rebels –boys just like himself – driven through the village streets and the women trilling and dancing. There was one image that seemed imprinted on his brain – the image of a Palestinian village woman. She had *red hair, blue eyes, and freckles*. She was waving her head shawl, dancing and trilling as the tears streamed down her face.

Chapter 34

The years are like seasons, Hasna reflected. *One has no sooner plowed the field and planted the seed when it is time to harvest the crop. A child has just been weaned; just learned to take his first tentative steps, when there is the shadow of a moustache on his upper lip. The horrible, wrenching grief that comes with the death of a child, the hanging of a youth, the reality of seeing the dead bodies of your two younger brothers in the back of a truck being driven through the streets become muted memories. The ache is still there, but the inconsolable, thob-renting grief is gone.*

This is life, Hasna sighed as she looked at her six, stalwart sons. They were now 16, 15, 13, 11, 9 and 8. *Abdallah would have been eighteen and ready for marriage; Saif and Ali would have had children of their own.* She often thought of them. They were as near as mind and heart.

There were no new babies in the house. The metal cradle had been stored in the *qa'albayt*. She was still hopeful that she might yet have a daughter, but it seemed it had not *been written* so. *I shall have to be content to find suitable wives for my sons,* she mused.

The events of the tragic years of the Arab Revolt were like the tattoos on the chins of elderly village women –

faded but indelibly printed – fine lines among the wrinkles – always *there* as visible reminders of the scars within.

There were still sporadic incidents, but nothing comparable to the horrendous occurrences of those turbulent years. The roads at times were unsafe, especially at night when snipers could be hidden beneath the trees. There were still occasional skirmishes between British soldiers of the Mandate and Palestinian Arabs; there were, ironically, growing confrontations between Zionist settlers and the Mandate government which had supported them during those troubled years. *Former allies had become enemies, or so it seemed,* Hasna thought.

One thing that can be said about us, Palestinians; we are adaptable! We have survived four hundred years of Turkish Occupation, decades of British Mandate, rumors that we would be transferred to Transjordan and our homes given to others. We adapt. We survive, Hasna sighed as she went about her work.

Again she looked at her six sons and *knew* how blessed she really was. Yes, there was poverty and hard work, but the sons of Adam were *made* for hard work – for trials and testing – so the Quran taught. It was not so much *what* happened to you, but *how* you dealt with it. Islam had taught her – had taught all of them – to say *illhumdillah* – to praise God for *everything* – the *bad* as well as the good. Islam taught not to *question*, but to have *faith* in the ultimate wisdom of Allah. When Hasna paused for prayer five times a day, she *always* asked for forgiveness for her doubt, for there *were* times that Hasna *did question.*

Hasna and the boys still sat on the stone stairs that climbed to the stars. No matter how big the boys had grown, they still seemed to enjoy these moments under the stars with their mother. The stories were not the same as they were when they were children. The boys loved tales about when their mother was young – though at thirty-one, Hasna was hardly old!

They would beg her to tell tales about her childhood. Hasna would always begin her tales with: *When-I-was-a-girl-and-not-very-pretty…* Issa, who was now eight, but not too big to sit in her lap, would raise his head from her shoulder and smile at her and very seriously say: "But you know you are really *beautiful.*" Hasna would chuckle and hug him. "You say that, *habeebee,* because you also have red hair, blue eyes and freckles!" Her older sons would protest in chorus, "But he is right, *Yum'ma* – you *are* beautiful!"

There were evenings when Mansur would join them on the stairs and listen to Hasna's tales. She was a wonderful storyteller. She had a knack of transforming ordinary events into an *adventure.* She would look into their rapt faces and say, "*ba'dane…* (and then…)"

They learned history; they learned customs and traditions; they learned religion and faith; they learned the fact that even though life was hard – sometimes horribly unjust and cruel – that there were lessons to be learned and that it was *not so much the event, but one's view of it.* They looked at their mother and how she had been molded by the events of her life – that *in spite* of all, she could laugh.

"I wonder what stories are written for each of you." Hasna would ponder looking into the dark eyes of Omar, Khalil, Kareem, Jameel, and Imad, giving blue-eyed Issa a hug. "I wonder what adventures each of you will have, my loves?"

The lights of Jerusalem could be seen in the distance; the lights from the watch tower of the Jewish settlement on the hilltop above cast tentative fingers of light down the hillside toward the village.

"It is getting chilly," Hasna said. "We should go down."

"Just *one* more story, *Yum'ma*. Please, just one more," Issa begged.

"One very, very *short one*," Hasna said as she kissed his red curls. "*When-I-was-a-girl-and-not- very pretty...*"

Coming 2016

The Well

A Palestinian saga- Book 2

The Well

Chapter 1

Omar watched the girl as she lowered the bucket into the well. He heard the echoing splash as the leather bucket hit the water. Bracing her bare feet on either side of the well, the girl hauled the bucket to the surface, pouring the clear water into the earthenware jar beside her. Drop…splash…pull. The girl repeated the pattern until the jar was full, water trickling over its rough brim, staining the sides of the clay vessel. Omar watched as she gracefully stooped and lifted the jug to her head. Her neck strained as it adjusted itself to the weight. Back erect, one arm raised in balancing the heavy water jar, the girl wound her way up the rocky path toward her home in the village.

Omar followed her with his eyes until her slender, erect shape vanished from view. He hadn't intended to spy on Nijmeh. He wasn't like some of the other boys who daily sat on the hill overlooking the well, hoping to catch sight of pretty girls, and if no women were present – whistling and hooting and calling to the girls drawing water. He had been searching for an errant lamb when he caught sight of her at the well. (As if to give legitimacy to his claim, he had the warm, wooly lamb nestled against his chest.) But when he saw her, he had concealed himself behind a thorn bush and watched; no better than a thirteen year old. He felt young and foolish and *guilty*. Nonetheless, there he was crouching on his knees praying that he wouldn't be seen.

Lately he'd been having disturbing dreams – dreams that caused him to twist and turn on his pallet and to lay awake long into the night while his brothers slept deeply around him -- dreams that caused him to awaken in the morning irritable and touchy and out of sorts with his brothers. Always in the dreams there was a face – a lovely, olive-skinned face – a face with sparkling black eyes outlined in kohl – a face framed with two thick raven plaits with bits of scarlet wool woven into the braid – the beautiful face of Nijmeh.

Omar's mother had been scolding him for months, ever since he turned seventeen that it was time for him to take a bride. Omar was the eldest of six brothers. He was tall and handsome; his body strong with the muscle that hard work in the fields brought. He had hair on his legs, hair on his arms and the beginning of curly hair on his chest. He was a man. His body told him so. His mother told him so.

"Omar," she said, "you should be married. You should do your duty and bring into the house a strong young wife who would help me with the work of this large family – a wife who would give me grandsons."

Omar had been resisting his mother's pressure. Partly because she was so insistent, mostly because he knew she had in mind his cousin, Miriam. He had known Miriam since they were children. She was like a sister who one knew was there, yet ignored. To Omar, Miriam was non-descript. She wasn't plain. She wasn't pretty. He really couldn't describe her if he had been asked point blank. He saw her at family gatherings helping her mother and aunts, lugging trays of food, or balancing her two year old brother on her hip. (When her mother wasn't looking, Omar had seen her box her brother's ears and then pinch him if he cried.) She was supposedly sweet and docile, and rarely spoke unless spoken to. Omar didn't know if this was because she was so well brought up, or if it was because she really had nothing to say. He rather suspected the latter. Omar knew his mother thought she would make a perfect wife: hardworking, quiet, well-mannered, and *obedient!* Those were the traits a mother looked for in a servant, or in a daughter-in-law. Someone she could control and manage. And Hasna liked to manage! They weren't the traits, however, that he looked for in a wife. As sweet as Miriam supposedly was, as hard-working as she assumingly might be, as quiet as she appeared, and as obedient as she may be – she didn't invade Omar's dreams or haunt his waking hours. Nijmeh did.

Nijmeh was also a relative (a point in Omar's favor), although distant; a member of the same *hamouleh* – clan. He had never had direct contact with her. He had never had direct contact with any girl. Not one word had passed between them; not one meaningful glance. Nothing. Perhaps, if Omar had had sisters, there would have been some chanced encounter with Nijmeh through them. But he lived in a world of men – except for Hasna – five brothers and his father. A man to have six sons was indeed a blessing from Allah as any Palestinian would say. But yet if he had had sisters he would have known something about girls. It was hard to know about girls from one's mother!

He didn't know much about Nijmeh other than that she was so beautiful his heart did funny dances when he saw her. He did know there weren't any brothers. She was the eldest of seven girls (an unfortunate adversity where the blessing of sons was praised). He did know that her father had died a few months ago (May God rest his soul) and that her mother was living with her husband's relatives. He had heard rumors that Nijmeh's uncles, burdened by the addition of eight more mouths to feed, were anxious to find suitable husbands for the two older girls. He did know where they could find a husband for the eldest, a husband who was tall and handsome and who bore a striking resemblance to *Omar*.

Hasna, Omar's mother, was sitting in the courtyard of their house preparing bread for the *taboon*. She patted each flat loaf between her floured hands then placed it on the tray of hot stones in the outdoor oven. As each loaf turned a rich, golden brown, she snatched it off and placed another flat loaf in its place. Her long sleeves were pushed up above her elbows and the long pointed part of the sleeves knotted and tied behind her neck so she could work. Her silver bracelets played a tune against each other as she molded the loaves made from the wheat she had grown and ground on the round stone mill.

Hasna was short and round, and when not ordering her sons about – quite jolly. She had inherited blue eyes and red hair from some Scottish Crusader who had left his gene pool when he returned to Europe from the Holy

Land. All of her sons were dark haired and dark eyed, except Issa, the youngest. He had unluckily inherited his mother's red hair, blue eyes, and a most impressive array of freckles.

"Yum'ma, I've been thinking about what you said," Omar began, tearing off a morsel of the rich, hot bread and bending down beside her on the stone floor. "I've been thinking about how you're always saying it's time for me to find a bride; time for me to bring a wife into our home to help you with the work."

Hasna paused in her shaping of the loaves. She looked at her handsome son – dark curls dusting his bronzed forehead, a day's growth of beard shadowing his cheeks, an impressive moustache shading his upper lip. Her heart turned over as it often did gazing at this, her first born. Though she loved all her sons with a passion bordering on idolatry (May God keep them and preserve them from harm), in the hidden recesses of her heart she knew that Omar was her favorite – with his flashing smile and loving nature and his captivating good looks. It was probably why she was so critical of him. She didn't want him to think too highly of himself, or her other sons to guess that he was her favorite. For him there must be a special bride – a girl of unrivaled worth – a girl who was quiet, well-mannered, hardworking and obedient – a maiden deserving such a prince like Omar. For him she had picked out his cousin, Miriam. A mother knew her son. A mother knew who would make him happy. Sons did not know (if they were to be given the chance to choose); mothers did!

From the time they were children, Hasna knew that Miriam was the mate for Omar. She would be the perfect wife for him. It had long been an understanding between the two families that when the age of puberty was reached (They did not want to rush these things as some families did); when the age for marriage was ripe (say sixteen or seventeen) Omar and Miriam would be wed.

"Ah, my son, my breath, my heart, at last you listen to an old woman's tongue. At last the words that I've poured into your ears for months have found fertile soil and taken root. Thank God. I will speak to your uncle's wife, Zareefeh, this very day. She has long awaited your desire to marry your cousin Miriam, as I have."

"Miriam? I don't want to marry Miriam! I've seen a girl..."

Hasna gasped, the temper that accompanied her red hair rushing to her tongue. "You've what! What does this mean, 'I've seen a girl?' Who gave you permission to see a girl? What kind of girl would allow herself to be seen by the likes of you?"

"*Yum'ma*, calm yourself. For months I've been dreaming of one girl. For weeks her face has come to me in my dreams at night and visited me in my thoughts during the day. I cannot eat because I think of her. I cannot dig in the field, but that I think of her. I cannot take the sheep and goats to graze, but that I think of her. *Yum'ma*, her face is like the moon. Her hair is black as the deepest night. Her eyes like two stars lighting the way for the traveler far from home. Whenever I think of her, I feel a great joy and a great longing. *Yum'ma*, I want to marry Nijmeh."

"Nijmeh? Who is this Nijmeh?" demanded Hasna.

"Nijmeh, *Yum'ma*, the daughter of Ahmad ibn Daoud. (May God rest his soul.)

"Nijmeh, *bint* Ahmad? The daughter of Azeezeh, your grandmother's cousin?"

"Yes, *Yum'ma*, *bint* Azeezeh."

"This is not possible my son. What do you want of Nijmeh? She is passably pretty, as you say, but she is not suitable for you. Your cousin, Miriam, now there is a maiden for you. Talk of beauty! Miriam. Talk of the moon and stars, and the blackness of night! Miriam. Talk of *suitableness* – Miriam. She has been saved for you since you were children. It is your father's wish, your uncle's wish, and it is *my wish* that when you marry, you marry Miriam. It has been settled long ago. Besides, I have heard that *bint* Ahmad's oldest girl is already spoken for. Abu Mahmoud has already sent the women of his family to sound out Azeezeh on Nijmeh's willingness."

"Abu Mahmoud!" Omar cried incredulously.

"Soon the men of his family," Hasna continued ignoring Omar's outburst, "will officially go and ask her hand from her uncles. Her uncles will agree.

People say that the girl may be somewhat reluctant because of Abu Mahmoud's age, and because he has so many children yet at home. But she realizes the burden she and her sisters are to their uncles. She will be convinced to do the expected thing. A girl like Nijmeh, without father or brothers, must not be too picky. Abu Mahmoud was her father's boyhood friend. His wife has been dead for forty days. He has waited the prescribed time before taking another wife. A man needs a woman to care for him and his children. He cannot be expected to do the work of a woman. Nijmeh can't hope to do better. Abu Mahmoud will make her a good husband. He will give her food, clothing, and a roof over her head."

"Abu Mahmoud! You can't be serious. Her uncles wouldn't permit this. Abu Mahmoud must be fifty. He is old enough to be Nijmeh's father or *grandfather!* She can't be given to Abu Mahmoud. It is unthinkable. He can't marry Nijmeh!"

"And who are you to have a say in this?" Hasna scolded. "Are you Nijmeh's uncle? Are you her brother? Are you her first cousin with a voice in this matter? The lambs do not decide where the rams are to graze. Especially the lamb from the neighbor's flock! These things are decided by the elders, by those blessed with the wisdom of experience and years, by those entrusted with the care of the family. You, my outspoken lamb, will be ruled by your father and uncle in the matter of marriage. You will be well-advised not to mention to your father your infatuation with Nijmeh *bint* Ahmad. He will not be as understanding and sympathetic as I have been. He wants you to marry his brother's daughter. He wants you to marry Miriam. And marry Miriam you will! You have told me all, haven't you?" Hasna paused. "You've not held back something I should know? You've not brought dishonor to your family with this girl, have you?"

Omar looked stunned at his mother's question and its implication. Anger and disbelief ignited in his eyes. "*Yum'ma*, how can you even ask me this? Am I not your son! Am I not the son of my father! Would I ever do anything to bring shame to our family's name? To myself? I have not spoken one word to Nijmeh. She knows nothing of my feelings."

Hasna reached up a rough, work-worn hand to her son's cheek. "I don't mean to be hard, my love. I know what you think you feel here," she whispered, placing her hand against his heart. "But this will pass. This is the shadow of love – seemingly beautiful, fragrant, a fire as it dances in your mind's eye. It is like the poppies that blanket the hillsides after the winter rains. They are beautiful and startling for a brief time, but soon they wither and droop and fade. So will what you think you feel for Nijmeh. Falling in love before marriage is foreign; it is an idea not to be trusted. Enduring love comes after marriage, not before. Love for Miriam will come. It will grow and blossom forth like the seed that is hidden in the earth pushes aside the pebble in its path and sprouts and matures into a sturdy tree. Dream of your cousin. Pepper your thoughts with visions of her. You and Nijmeh --that is a dream which will never be. Accept what cannot be changed."

Omar tried to do what his mother said. She was a forceful, domineering woman. For seventeen years he had been under her thumb. As he laid on his pallet that night, next to his brother, Khalil, as he listened to the sounds of his little brothers moving in their sleep, he could not push the vision of Nijmeh from his mind. He *would not* replace it with the picture of Miriam. He *could not*. He would not! He was seventeen. He was strong. He was a man, not a lamb blindly following the ewe. He would not give up so easily, despite what his mother said. He would find a way to marry Nijmeh.

About the Author

Donn Hutchison first came to Palestine, from small town Pennsylvania, as part of a student teaching program. He became a legal citizen of the Israeli occupied West Bank when a census was carried out after the Six Day War and he was counted as a resident. Palestine became his home. He continued to teach English to Palestinian youth, married, and raised his children in the occupied city of Ramallah where he still resides. Donn has had articles published in "Quaker Life", "This Week in Palestine", and "The Jerusalem Quarterly" magazines. In addition to his first hand experiences, he has been privy to a wealth of stories recounted by generations of Palestinians who lived and raised their families in the region throughout its turbulent history. His goal is to give his audience an idea of what life was like in Palestine through the eyes of this wonderful fictional family.

ACKNOWLEDGEMENTS

I am grateful to my mother-in-law, Ellen Audi Mansur, who made the end of the four hundred year Ottoman rule and the years of the British Mandate come alive for me through her stories.

I am indebted to Carol Hutchison Vago who read the chapters as they were written and gave instant feedback, often critical, always insightful, and always supportive.

I am pleased to give credit to Anan Barghouti for the use of his photograph on the cover: the Palestinian hills, the rough arch, and the stone steps leading to the stars.

I wish to thank those family and friends who read sample chapters and complete drafts for their encouragement.

I am grateful for all the work of Rana Hutchison Copeland. Without her prompting, encouragement, rereading, and researching: *how to go about self-publishing*, the manuscripts would continue to be in the *bottom dresser drawer.*